WHERE SHE
BRUSHED HER HAIR

and Other Stories

WHERE SHE BRUSHED HER HAIR

AND OTHER STORIES

---

by Max Steele

HARPER & ROW, PUBLISHERS
New York, Evanston, and London

The stories in this volume originally appeared in the following publications: "The Cat and the Coffee Drinkers," *The New Yorker;* "Captain of the White Yacht," "The Wanton Troopers," "The Glass-Brick Apartment," "Hereby Hangs a Tale," and "Promiscuous Unbound," *Harper's Magazine;* "Big Goat, Little Goat," *Mademoiselle;* "The Rescue," *Cosmopolitan;* "A Caracole in Paris," *New Mexico Quarterly;* "Hear the Wind Blow," *Discovery;* "From the French Quarter," *Esquire;* "The Year of the Lily-Blight," *Transatlantic Review*; "What to Do Till the Postman Comes," *Paris Review;* "Where She Brushed Her Hair" (originally titled "Fiction, Fact and Dream"), *Carolina Quarterly.*

LIBRARY OF CONGRESS CATALOG CARD NUMBER: 67-28821

B-S

For her family and friends
in memory of
Jessie Rehder

Contents

THE CAT AND THE
COFFEE DRINKERS

I sometimes wonder if the generation of mothers who from 1910 to 1940 sent their five-year-olds to the kindergarten of Miss Effie Barr had much of an idea what their children were learning in her one-room schoolhouse. Even though in 1930 the Southern town in which she lived was no longer small, and even though she was already in her seventies, Miss Effie knew all of the children in her school a year, and often longer, before they appeared before her for lessons. My mother, properly gloved and chapeaued, began taking me to call on her when I was four.

Her house was a good place to visit. It was large and gray, and was set well back from the same street that I lived on. It was the last "white" house before the Negro part of town, and the first Negro houses had been, up until the depression, part of the Barr properties. There were mossy brick steps leading from a hitching post up to a gravel walk that curved between overgrown boxwoods to a low porch with twelve slender columns. There, in the summer, in the shade of water oaks, Miss Effie, dressed in black, would be sitting, knitting or embroidering, while her big gray cat sat at, and sometimes on, her feet. Slow, uncertain music would be coming through open windows from the music room, where her older sister, Miss Hattie, gave piano lessons.

Miss Effie never seemed to watch a child on such visits, or offer him anything like cookies or lemonade, or say anything to endear herself to a youngster. Instead, she would talk lady talk with the mother and, hardly pausing, say to the child, "You can pull up the wild onions on the lawn if you've nothing better to do." There was no suggestion in her voice that it was a game or that there would be a reward. She simply stated what could be done if one took a notion. Usually a child did.

There was no nonsense about Miss Effie. One morning in late September, my mother and I were standing with eleven other mothers and children on the porch. Miss Effie looked everyone over carefully from where she stood with one hand on the screen door. She checked a list in the other hand against the young faces on the porch, to be sure that these were the children she had chosen from the forty or more who had visited her in the summer. Apparently satisfied, or at least reconciled to another year of supplementing her income (for no Southern lady of her generation "worked"), she opened the door wide and said, in her indifferent tone, "Children inside." When one mother tried to lead her reluctant son into the dark parlor, Miss Effie said, "Mothers outside."

When the children were all inside and the mothers outside, Miss Effie latched the screen, thanked the mothers for bringing the children, and reminded them that classes began at eight-thirty and ended at noon. The tuition, two dollars a week, would be acceptable each Friday, and each child, as part of his training, should be given the responsibility of delivering the money in an envelope bearing the parent's signature. She thanked the mothers again in such a way that there was nothing for them to do except wander together in a group down the gravel walk.

Miss Effie then turned to us, who were standing somewhat closer together than was necessary, in the center of the dark parlor, and said, "Since this is your first day, I want to show you everything. Then you won't be wondering about things while you should be listening."

She made us look at the Oriental carpet, the grandfather's clock, the bookcases of leatherbound volumes, the shelves on which were collections of rocks, shells, birds' nests, and petrified wood. She offered to let us touch, just this once, any of these things.

She would not let us into the music room, which was then empty, but indicated through the doorway the imported grand piano, the red plush seat where Miss Hattie sat during lessons, the music racks, the ferns, and the window seats, which she said were full of sheet music. "You're never to go in there," she said. "I don't go in there myself."

Next, she showed us the dining room, the den, and the hallway, and at the foot of the stairs she said, "We're going upstairs, and then you'll never go up there again." Barbara Ware, one of three girls in our class, began to whimper. "Don't worry," Miss Effie said, "you'll come back down. But there'll be no reason to go up again. I want you to see everything, so you won't have to ask personal questions, which would certainly be the height of impoliteness, wouldn't it? I mean, if you started wanting to know, without my telling you, where I sleep and which window is Miss

Hattie's, I'd think you were rude, wouldn't I? I'll show you everything, so you won't be tempted to ask personal questions."

We went upstairs, and she showed us her room and where she kept her shoes (in the steps leading up to the side of her fourposter bed), where she hung her clothes (in two large armoires) and kept her hatbox (in a teakwood sea chest). The cat, she said, slept on the sea chest if he happened to be home at night.

She then knocked on the door of Miss Hattie's room and asked her sister, who was inside, if we might look in. Miss Hattie agreed to a short visit. After that, Miss Effie showed us the upstairs bathroom and explained that the bathtub faucet dripped all night and that was why a towel was kept under it.

Downstairs again, Miss Effie let us see the "new" kitchen, which was built in 1900, and the back porch, which had been screened in only four years before, and which had a small door through which the cat could come and go as he liked. We were as fascinated by everything as we would have been if we had never seen a house before.

"Now, out the back door. All of you." She made us all stand on the ground, off the steps, while she lowered herself, step by step, with the aid of a cane that she kept on a nail by the door. "Now you've seen my house and you won't see it again. Unless I give your mothers fruitcake and coffee at Christmas. And I don't think I will. Not this year. Do you ever get tired of fruitcake and coffee at Christmas?"

We said we did, since it was clear that she did.

"Over there is the barn, and we'll see it some other time, and that is the greenhouse, and we'll be seeing it often. And here is the classroom, where we'll be." She pointed with her cane to a square brick building that before the

Civil War had been the kitchen. The door was open.

She shepherded us along a brick walk with her cane, not allowing any of us near enough to her to topple her over. At the door, she said, "Go on in."

We crowded in, and when we were all through the door she summoned us back out. "Now, which of you are boys?" The nine boys raised their hands, following her lead. "And which girls?" The three girls had already separated themselves from the boys, and nodded together. "All right, then, young gentlemen," she said, regarding us, "let's let the young ladies enter first. Or I may think you're all young ladies."

The girls, looking timid and pleased, entered. We started in after them.

"Wait just a minute, young gentlemen," she said. "Haven't you forgotten something?" We looked about for another girl.

"Me!" she announced. "You've forgotten me!" She passed through our huddle, separating us with her stick, and marched into the kitchen.

Inside, as well as out, the kitchen was mainly of brick. The walls and floor were brick, and the hearth and the huge chimney, except for a closet-cupboard on each side of it, were brick. The ceiling, however, was of beams and broad boards, and the windows were of wavy glass in casements that opened out like shutters. There were three large wooden tables, and at each table four chairs.

Again she had to show us everything. The fireplace would be used in only the coldest weather, she said. At other times, an iron stove at one side of the room would be used. A captain's chair, between the fireplace and the stove, was her own and not to be touched by us. A sewing table, overflowing with yarn and knitting needles, was for her own use, and not for ours. One cupboard, the one near her, held dishes. She opened its door. She would let us see in the other cupboard later. The tables and chairs and, at the far end of the room, some pegs for coats were all ours, to do with as we pleased. It was, she explained, our school-room, and therefore, since we were young ladies and gen-tlemen, she was sure we would keep it clean.

As a matter of fact, she saw no reason why we should not begin with the first lesson: Sweeping and Dusting. She opened the other cupboard and showed us a mop, a bucket, some rags and brushes, and three brooms. We were not divided into teams; we were not given certain areas to see who could sweep his area cleanest; we were simply told that young ladies should naturally be able to sweep and that young gentlemen at some times in their lives would certainly be expected to sweep a room clean.

The instruction was simple: "You get a good grip on the handle and set to." She handed out the three brooms and started us boys sweeping from the fireplace toward the front door. She made simple corrections: "You'll raise a dust, flirting the broom upward. Keep it near the floor." "Hold lower on the handle. You'll get more dirt." "Don't bend over. You'll be tired before the floor is clean."

When we swept, Miss Effie made a big red enamel cof-feepot of coffee on a small alcohol stove. Since the room had not been swept, she admitted, all summer, there was a respectable pile of brick dust, sand, and sweepings near the door by the time she said, "We'll have lunch now." It was already ten o'clock. "After lunch, I'll teach you how to take up trash and to dust. Everyone needs to know that."

"Lunch," it happened, was half a mug of coffee each. One spoon of sugar, she said, was sufficient if we felt it necessary to use sugar at all (she didn't); there was milk for those who could not or would not (she spoke as though using milk were a defect of character) take their coffee black. I daresay not any of us had ever had coffee before, and Robert Barnes said he hadn't.

"Good!" Miss Effie said. "So you have learned something today."

Miriam Wells, however, said, on reflection, that her parents wouldn't approve of her drinking coffee.

"Very well," Miss Effie said. "Don't drink it. And the next time I offer you any, if I ever do, simply say 'No, thank you, Ma'am.' " (The next day, Miriam Wells was drinking it along with the rest of us.) "Let's get this clear right this minute—your parents don't need to know what you do when you're under my instruction."

Her firm words gave us a warm feeling, and from that moment on the schoolroom became a special, safe, and rather secret place.

That day, we learned, further, how to rinse out mugs and place them in a pan to be boiled later, how to take up trash, and how to dust. At noon, we were taught the right way to put on our sweaters or coats, how to approach, one at a time, our teacher (or any lady we should happen to be visiting) and say "Thank you" (for the coffee or whatever we had been served), and how to say goodbye and turn and leave the room without running or laughing. It wasn't as easy as you may think.

The next morning, Robert Barnes was waiting on his steps when I walked by his house. Since he and I lived nearer to the Barrs' than any of the other children, we were the first to arrive at the schoolhouse.

Miss Effie sat in her captain's chair brushing the cat, which lay on a tall stool in front of her. We entered without speaking. Without looking up, Miss Effie said, "Now, young gentlemen, let's try that again—outside. Take off your caps before you step through the door, and say 'Good morning, Ma'am' as you come through the door. Smile if you feel like it. Don't if you don't." She herself did not smile as we went out and re-entered in the manner she suggested. However, this time she looked directly at us when she returned our "Good mornings." Later, each child who entered the room in what she felt to be a rude way was sent out to try again.

Strangely enough, she did not smile at anyone, and looking back I see now that part of her efficiency was that she treated each child as an adult and each lesson as though it were a serious task. Even though there were occasional crying scenes or temper tantrums among us, she herself never lost her firm, rational approach. Sitting in her captain's chair, dressed in black from neck to toe, except for a cameo, small gold loop earrings, and a gold opal ring on her right hand, she was usually as solemn and considerate as a judge on his bench. It is strange that I can remember her calm expression and the dignity of her bearing, but not one feature of her angular face.

That morning, Miss Effie waited until all of us were properly in before addressing us as a class. "This is Mr. Thomas," she said of the cat on the stool. "He's a no-good cat and he doesn't like children, so leave him alone. I'd have nothing to do with him myself except that he happens to belong to me because his mother and grandmother belonged to me. They were no good, either. But since he does belong to me and since he is here, we may as well talk about cats."

She showed us how to brush a cat, how he liked to be rubbed under his neck, how he didn't like his ears or whiskers touched, how his ears turned to pick up sounds, how he stretched and shut his paw pads when he was tickled on the stomach or feet, and how he twitched his tail when annoyed. "Mr. Thomas is a fighter," she said, and let us look at the scars from a dozen or more fights, "and he's getting too old to fight, but he hasn't got sense enough to know that."

She looked at us where we stood in more or less a large

circle around her. "Now, let's see, I don't know your names. I know your mothers, but not your names." She would, she said, indicate us one at a time and we were to give our names in clear, loud voices while looking her right in the eye. Then we were to choose a chair at one of the three tables. "I hate the way most people become shy when they say their names. Be proud of it and speak up."

When the young ladies had finished giving their names, she said they did admirably well; they chose to sit at the same table. One or two boys shouted their names in a silly fashion and had to repeat. One or two looked away, to decide on a chair or to watch the cat, they claimed, and so had to repeat. I did not speak loud enough and had to say my name three times. One lad refused to say his name a second time, and that day and the next she called him Mr. No-Name. The third day afterward, he did not appear, nor the fourth nor fifth, and the next week a new boy from the waiting list gave his name in a perfect fashion and took Mr. No-Name's place.

We learned about cats and names the second day, then. The following day, Barbara Ware and Robert Barnes distinguished themselves by claiming to like their coffee black with no sugar, just the way Miss Effie was convinced it should be drunk.

At the end of the second week, we reviewed what we had learned by sweeping and dusting the room again. And each day we practiced coming in and leaving properly and saying our name in a way that sounded as though we were proud of it and of ourselves—which by then we were.

The third week, putting down the cat brush and shooing Mr. Thomas off the stool, Miss Effie said that she, too, was proud of the way we identified ourselves with eyes level and unblinking. "But now," she said, "I want to teach you to give a name that is not your own. Without any shiftiness."

She sat with both thin hands clasping the arms of her

chair and gave a short lecture. Not everyone, she said, was entitled to know your name. Some people of a certain sort would ask when it was none of their business. It would be unnecessarily rude to tell them so. But we could simply tell such people a name that had nothing whatever to do with our own. She did not mention kidnapings, but talked rather about ruthless salesmen, strangers on buses and trains, and tramps and beggars wandering through the neighborhood.

For the purpose of practice, all of the young ladies would learn to give, in a courteous, convincing manner, the name "Polly Livingstone." The boys would be, when asked, "William Johnson" (a name I can still give with much more conviction than my own). That day and the next, each of us gave his real name before the coffee break, and after coffee his false name. We liked the exercises wherein we went up to her, shook her hand if she offered it, and gave our false names, confronting, without staring, her solemn gaze with ours. If we smiled, or twisted, we had to stand by the fireplace until we could display more poise.

At the end of the first month, Miss Effie said that she was fairly well pleased with our progress. "I have taught you, thus far, mainly about rooms. Most people spend most of their lives in rooms, and now you know about them." She mentioned some of the things we had learned. "What else have we learned about rooms?" she then asked, letting Mr. Thomas out the window onto the sunny ledge where he liked to sit.

"How to drink coffee," Miriam Wells said, rather proudly.

"No," Miss Effie said, "that has to do with another series, which includes how to accept things and how to get rid of things you don't want—fat meat, bones, seeds, pits, peelings, and [she added under her breath] parents." She paused for a moment and looked pleased, as though she

might wink or smile, but her angular face did not change
its expression very much. "No. Besides, I'm not pleased
with the way you're drinking coffee." She then said for the
first time a speech that she repeated so often that by the
end of the year we sometimes shouted it in our play on the
way home. "Coffee is a beverage to be enjoyed for its
flavor. It is not a food to be enriched with milk and sugar.
Only certain types of people try to gain nourishment from
it. In general, they are the ones, I suspect, who show their
emotions in public." (We had, I'm sure, no idea what the
speech meant.) She expected all of us by June, possibly by
Christmas, to be drinking it black. "Is there anything else
we need to know about rooms?" she asked.

"How to build them," Phillip Pike said.

"That," Miss Effie said, "you can't learn from me. Un-
fortunately. I wish I knew." She looked thoughtfully out
the window to the ledge on which Mr. Thomas was groom-
ing himself. "Windows!" she said. "How to clean windows."

Again the cupboard was opened, and by noon the next
day we knew how to clean windows, inside and out, and
how to adjust all the shades in a room to the same level.

When it turned cold in November, cold enough for the
stove but not the fireplace, we settled down to the real
work that gave Miss Effie's kindergarten its reputation.
Reading. Miss Effie liked to read, and it was well known in
the town and especially among the public-school teachers
that the two or three hundred children she had taught had
grown up reading everything they could find. She assured
us that even though we were only five years old, we would
be reading better than the third-grade schoolchildren by
the end of the year.

Each morning, the stove was already hot when we arrived. She would brush Thomas awhile, and then, when we
were all in our places and warm, she would hand out our
reading books, which we opened every day to the first

page and laid flat before us on the tables. While we looked at the first page, she began heating the big red enamel pot of coffee, and also, because we now needed nourishment to keep warm, a black iron pot of oatmeal. Then Miss Effie would sit down, allow Thomas to jump into her lap, and begin reading, always from the first page, in an excited tone. She would read to the point exactly where we had finished the day before, so that from necessity she read faster each day, while we turned our pages, which we knew by heart, when we saw her ready to turn hers.

Then, one after another, we went up to her and sat on Mr. Thomas's stool by the stove and read aloud to her while those at the tables either listened or read or played with architectural blocks. The child on the stool was rewarded at the end of each sentence with two spoonfuls of oatmeal if he read well, one if not so well. Since we each read twice, once before coffee and once after, we did not really get hungry before we left the school at noon. Of course, those who read fast and well ate more oatmeal than the others.

In addition to the reading lessons, which were the most important part of the day, we learned to take money and shopping lists to Mr. Zenacher's grocery store, to pay for groceries, and to bring them back with the change. Usually two or three of us went together to the store, which was in the next block. At the same time, three or four others might be learning to paint flowerpots or to catch frying-size chickens in the chicken yard back of the barn.

On sunny days that winter, we would all go out to the greenhouse for an hour and learn to reset ferns and to start bulbs on wet beds of rock. In March, we learned how to rake Miss Effie's tennis court, to fill in any holes with powdery sand, and to line up and tie strings properly so that later a Negro yardman could mark the lines on the court with lime. The tennis court was for rent to high-school girls and boys in the afternoons during the spring and summer.

By Easter time, we were all proficient sweepers, dusters, shoppers, bulb-setters, readers, and black-coffee drinkers. Miss Effie herself, now that spring was in the air, hated to sit all morning by the stove, where we'd been all winter. Usually, after an hour or so of reading, all aloud and at once, we would follow her into the yard and prune the "first-breath-of-spring," the jessamine, the yellow bells, and the peach and pear trees. We kept the branches we cut off and we stuck them in buckets of water in the greenhouse. Miss Effie printed a sign that said "Flowers for Sale," and we helped her tie it to a tree near the sidewalk. In addition to the flowering branches that we had forced, she sold ferns and the jonquils that we had set and that were now in bud.

All in all, spring was a busy time. And I remember only one other thing we learned. One warm May morning, we arrived to find Mr. Thomas, badly torn about the ears, his eyes shut, his breathing noisy, on a folded piece of carpet near the open door of the schoolhouse. We wanted to pet him and talk to him, but Miss Effie, regarding him constantly, said no, that he had obviously been not only a bad cat but a foolish one. She believed he had been hit by a car while running from some dogs, and that that was how the dogs got to him. (She and Miss Hattie had heard the fight during the night.) At any rate, he had managed to crawl under the steps, where the dogs couldn't get to him any more. At dawn she had come down and thrown hot water on the dogs and rescued him.

As soon as a Negro boy from her cousin's office arrived (her cousin was a doctor), she was going to teach us how to put a cat to sleep, she said.

We pointed out that he already seemed to be asleep.

"But," she explained, not taking her eyes from the cat, "we are going to put him to sleep so that he won't wake up."

"You're going to kill him?" Robert Barnes said.

"You could say that."

We were all greatly disturbed when we understood that this was the last we would see of Mr. Thomas. But Miss Effie had no sympathy, apparently, for the cat or for us. "He is suffering, and even if he is a no-good cat, he shouldn't suffer." When Barbara Ware began to whimper, Miss Effie said, "Animals are not people." Her tone was severe enough to stop Barbara from crying.

After the Negro boy had arrived with the package and left, Miss Effie stopped her reading, and, going to one of the cupboards, she got out a canvas bag with a drawstring top. "Now, if you young ladies will follow us, I'll ask the young gentlemen to bring Mr. Thomas."

We all rushed to be the ones to lift the piece of carpet and bear Mr. Thomas after her, through her garden, to the tool shed.

"Just wrap the carpet around him. Tight. Head and all," she instructed when we reached the tool shed.

After we had him wrapped securely, Miss Effie opened the package and read the label: "Chloroform." She explained to us the properties of the chemical while we rolled the cat tighter and stuck him, tail first, into the canvas bag. Miss Effie asked us to stand back and hold our breath. She then soaked a large rag with the liquid and poured the rest directly onto the cat's head and on the carpet. She poked the rag into the rolled carpet so that it hid Mr. Thomas completely. She then drew the drawstring tight and slung the cat, bag and all, into the tool shed. She shut the door firmly and latched it. "That'll cut out the air," she said.

Back in the schoolhouse, we tried to listen as she read,

without her usual excited tone, but we were all thinking about Mr. Thomas in the tool shed.

"Well," she finally said, "if you will excuse me a moment, I'll go see if my cat is dead."

We watched from the windows as she walked with her cane through the garden to the tool shed. We could see her open the door and bend over the sack for a long time. At last, she straightened up and locked the door again. She came back with the same unhalting gait and stood for a moment in the sun before the open door of the schoolhouse.

"When I dismiss you, you're to go straight home. And if they want to know why you're home early"—she stopped and studied the ground as though she had lost there her cameo or her words—"tell them the only thing Miss Effie had to teach you today was how to kill a cat."

Without waiting for us to leave, she walked in her usual dignified fashion down the brick walk and up the back steps and into her house, shutting the kitchen door firmly behind her. I know that that was not the last day of school, for I remember helping to spread tablecloths over the reading tables, and I remember helping to serve teacakes to the mothers who came the last day and stood on the tennis court near a table where Miss Hattie was serving coffee. But the final, definite picture I have of Miss Effie is that of her coming through the garden from the tool shed and standing in the doorway a moment to say that she had nothing more to teach us.

CAPTAIN OF
THE WHITE YACHT

———

An island, to be sure, is a timeless place. But these sand-banks off the Carolina shores are as involved with time as one is with a memory which threatens to quiver with life. A stranger has the same feeling here he might have when he awakes at twilight and finds that the watch on his wrist has stopped and the only clue from the gray sky through the window is that it is either dusk or dawn. But then the stranger hears the commanding ticking of the hall clock and the wonder becomes agony. Somewhere order exists and he cannot lie pleasantly on his back perusing the opalescent sky and choosing at will either dawn or dusk.

Perhaps the natives whose families have existed on the outerbanks for a hundred years and longer are not time-haunted. Perhaps in their hall they have a different clock which the stranger cannot see or hear: a clock which keeps a secret time. They tell you in their Old England accents:

"Hoi toide comes noigh touching the light'ouse now. Ere it was a moil away." And "ere" may mean either yesterday or two hundred years ago. An island is timeless and constant; on the outerbanks the shorelines shift with the seasons and within a man's lifetime he may surf fish where he once hunted golden pheasants and chased wild ponies. He may build a house where once he launched a boat.

Thus the changing sea gradually ate into the land and threatened the lighthouse; thus a tower with the new light was built in the low pine hills above Baxter, a mile away from the old lighthouse and the inconstant sea. A light a mile away from the lighthouse, one would think, could easily have been confusing to unchartered boats, but every day ships passed safely in Punto Sound and on the Atlantic —every day except one.

Late on that September evening before good dark, four men from Little Mitty Mitchell saw a white yacht approaching. It was a beautiful craft, a pleasure boat. They watched a moment. Certainly it was steering directly toward an underwater sandbar that had begun twisting two miles offshore. The four men waved her back with a canvas top from the sand-stalled jeep. They shouted desperately and ridiculously and still the white yacht steered true toward the treacherous sandbar. In Little Mitty Mitchell they heard the shouting and the younger men came running. The older people and the children hurried down after them with lanterns and torches and with the long rope and rusty first-aid tin. The young men waved the lanterns and ran up and down the twilit beach near the black ocean. The vessel moved slowly on a straight course. The old people huddled together on the soft sand, talking low, looking not at each other but at the imperiled craft. Gradually and then suddenly they ceased their murmuring and were silent. The white yacht was no longer moving. The young men stopped their running, stopped their signaling. An old sailor ran down to the water-edge and tried to shout in a rasping voice above the hollow roar of the surf.

Soon it was good dark. A beach fire was blazing and the tall sandgrass was dancing brightly on the dunes behind the still natives. Family at a time left to eat and returned to wait. They brought back coffee which they kept boiling in a bucket half buried in the ashes. They lay in the sand drinking coffee and later cold ale and recalling the hundred and more boats that had sunk during storms and wars at Star Point. They sat up wondering again why the yacht had not yet sent out a boat. Some of the younger men argued that they should go out to her, but the older men who had been sailors and coast guardsmen pointed out wisely that that would be work and that she was obviously not disabled. Wait, they said, if the skipper wants help he'll send for it. Wait. It would indeed be work: they waited.

Pickard, the strong and foolish golden retriever, bounded up the beach and barked at the darkness. Rushed back by a stampede of following phantoms he circled the fire once, then suddenly flopped, and gazed thoughtfully at the dying fire. The night was powdery with starlight; the flames were thinning blue over the bright coals; and far out on the ocean the sole light stared coldly at the shore.

"I believe the damn fool's dying." The voice sounded deep and resonant on the night air. The fire-flickering faces turned up the beach toward the night voice, frowning to hear more. The silly dog yawned and shut his eyes. Keppin Devron whispered what he had heard: "I believe the damn fool's dying." The others nodded yes indeed.

First his white cap, then his white trousers appeared, then his face and the gold buttons on his dark jacket. He strode briskly to the beach fire in long elegant strides. "Has anyone a cigarette?" It was more a command than a request. He glanced quickly down at the curious faces and dismissed them immediately. With a thin, engraved lighter he lit the cigarette that a skull-faced man handed him, drew once deeply, blew smoke over the stars, and said again: "I believe the damn fool's dying." The faces questioned.

"The ship's cook. Up the beach." He jerked his head backward. "Is there a doctor on this place?"

Keppin Devron began explaining that during the last year of the war a naval doctor who had lost a leg in an explosion had arrived and was now living. . . . "Better take him to the doctor. He's down the beach. About a half-mile."

Without a word the four MacMillan brothers, already in their jeep, raced on the hard sand up the beach. The captain shifted the large flat case under his arm. "I want to be taken to the nearest coast guard station. I'm on a sandbar."

Keppin Devron offered to drive him the four miles up the inside-rut. Together they walked toward the tar-painted A-model. Underfoot the soft sand whispered.

At the coast guard station, a ridiculous old Victorian house on a lonely stretch of sand, the captain strode without knocking into the smoky station and announced: "I'd like for you to send for the cutter."

The old coast guard lieutenant stood and questioned with his squinted eyes.

"I need the cutter immediately."

"The cutter is at Charleston. What do you want it for?"

"I'm on your goddamn sandbar."

"I have no sandbar." The lieutenant spoke firmly.

Keppin Devron intervened with his good-natured voice and laughing eyes: "The one you're plotting on the new chart. Out from Little Mitty. Up from Star Point."

The lieutenant asked when and where and why and how; and why the coast guard had not been notified immediately. The captain presented his card and pronounced the name: "Shaffer Daniel Cadenhead." He did not seem willing to say more to the men who were gathering close around.

A hullabaloo cleared the smoke. Cadenhead listened
carefully to each man and waited until all curiosity was ut-
tered before letting a muscle relax in his hard face. He considered well before answering in a flat and final tone. He
had set sail from Boston. Yes, he owned the yacht outright.
Had bought it three months ago with money left by his first
wife. At that time the craft was insured for $100,000. Now
there was no insurance covering her. He had refused to
sell her for $123,500 before leaving Boston. She had a sev-
enty-ton keel. The charter was for Bermuda. Early that
day the cook had doubled over in cramps. Appendicitis un-
doubtedly. Probably ruptured by now. Naturally he had to
be put ashore. Before dark they had sighted the lighthouse.
A few minutes later when the light came on they seemed
to be off course. Cadenhead himself had taken the wheel
for correction. The ship had struck the sandbar and stuck
fast. He would attempt nothing more until the cutter arrived. Now he was hungry.

A befreckled lad disappeared and returned with a hot
plate of fried fish, cheese, big biscuits, and bitter black
coffee steaming in a huge cup. Cadenhead opened the case
which he had been holding under his arm and inspected
the purple velvet and the ornate silverware before choosing
a knife, fork, and spoon—unaware of the men who stood
watching in an amused yet respectful awe.

At dawn, at the very instant the sun burst from the
sea, Cadenhead was walking to the top of the tall sand-
fence to stare out toward Star Point where the white
yacht lay motionless on the brilliant water. The old
beach fire and ale cans had been night-buried by the
high tide and now dry sand was washing over them. Deli-
cately, stealthily, the sand traced the creases of his white
shoes, then lavished them completely.

It was a solemn yet festive morning. By noon most of
the natives of Little Mitty had come down and now men

were coming from Mitty Mitchell, Cornwallis, and even from as far as Hesperes. Some had come to see the yacht, and others had come apurpose to see the captain who ate with his own silverware. Cadenhead stood on the sand dune above the beach and refused with curt but civil answers to be engaged in conversation.

By afternoon a herd of old jeeps and A-model Fords with slick balloon tires were standing on the beach, their motors pointing upwind away from the blowing sand. The fish were biting and the natives were already forgetting the plight of the yacht. Cadenhead alone was not fishing. Standing on a high dune and momentarily turning his eyes from the yacht, he caught sight of the Negro walking slowly up the beach. "Why in hell aren't you dead?"

"I didn't have appendicitis," the Negro called. "Stomach-ache was all."

Cadenhead poised until the Negro was close below him. Then he sprang and knocked him to the ground, falling with him, hitting him in the face with his fist, and rolling with him to the bottom of the dune. "You sonovabitch. I'll kill you." They rolled in the sand. Cadenhead swung a hard fist and cracked the Negro's eye socket. The Negro's huge hand closed on his throat. Cadenhead kicked free, leaped to his feet. The Negro tackled him. Breathlessly they struggled together and stood up gripping desperately. "I'll kill you," Cadenhead gasped. The Negro tore clean, ran up the beach, disappeared over a sand dune. Cadenhead sank to his knees; his coat sleeve, torn at the shoulder seam, hung down over the knuckles of his elegant bony hands. Blood dripped steadily from his nostrils and stained the white sand and one knee. He ignored the natives who offered him medicine or bandages, and brandy. When finally he raised his head, he stared only at the white yacht.

The following day the cutter arrived—and left. Caden-head had coldly demanded ridiculous help. He expected the cutter to approach his ship through the treacherous sandbars, which they could not hope to do successfully. They would throw out long lines and try tugging her free. But Cadenhead knew a craft could be wrenched apart by long lines. The coast guard officers refused to sign a statement which would make the coast guard responsible for all damages done to the vessel during the attempted rescue work. Cadenhead, now in a cold temper, revealed his first plan: he would open a suit against the coast guard for giving inadequate information about the coast and the separation of the light from the lighthouse. The officers informed him about the sources of quite adequate information. "We'll let the courts decide," Cadenhead announced. The officers said in such a case they could not touch the yacht. "Then get out!" Cadenhead ordered.

The yacht's crew, listening to the quarrel, demanded release and pay; Cadenhead said they could not quit, said wait, wait until he could phone a salvaging company in Wilmington. Wait. The crew waited. Cadenhead phoned. The small company had one job on hand but ten days later the salvaging tugs and barges appeared. A week passed before Cadenhead came ashore again. He had not shaved and his white shoes and trousers were oil-stained. Looking directly at nothing he marched to Mr. Billy's Grocery. He ordered ten pounds of corn meal, ten pounds of white beans, eight pounds of streaked bacon, and a dozen bottles of ketchup.

Then, although he had not been asked, he turned and faced the natives, who were sitting on wall-benches near the soda fountain, and explained: "The sand is silting around the keel faster than they can move it." He had signed a contract for $10,000 with the company but he did not have much faith in them. The owners, two ex-GI's, were sinking tanks, securing them to the ship, emptying them of water and pumping them full of air. But the tanks barely budged the yacht, barely made it tremble. Of course,

Cadenhead smiled; if they did not free the ship the contract would be broken, whether they knew it or not, without a penny paid. As he spoke his eyes sighted every person in the store before stopping hypnotically on Keppin Devron and Rona Bruton who sat close together, their hands touching. Finally Keppin Devron, the laugh-wrinkles deepening about his faded blue eyes, spoke: "You're wasting your time and their money."

Cadenhead blazed: "How do you know?"

"We've had a storm and three high seas since she's been out there. I know what a storm does to that ocean floor. If the ocean can't float her, you can't. Each of those seas has buried that hull even more."

Cadenhead smiled. "You may be right." He gazed deliberately at Rona, who clung quickly to Keppin Devron. He picked up his bundles and left, still smiling.

Now October can be a bitter month on the banks. Obsessed hurricane winds whirl near and push the ocean over the banks into the sound and then draw it back again, cutting gullies and channels across the island roads while the natives locked inside their houses battle the salt-sprayed wind which threatens them at every sash. The coast guard began to warn of an approaching twister. Maddened by the imminent danger to their equipment, the two GI's demanded release. Cadenhead would not listen. "We'll save her. We've got to save her. During the high seas we'll free her. There'll be a bonus. Hear me. A bonus." The GI's, as though paralyzed at sight of this desperate man, and perhaps wanting to believe that the rough sea might be a boon, waited. The hurricane whipped in, blinding, unleashing a fury that ripped across the yacht taking wood and brass superstructure with it. The barge with all the salvaging equipment and then the tug broke loose and within sight of the yacht were dashed under the waves. After the storm Cadenhead walked the yacht's deck writing in a ledger the considerable damage done; deaf to the GI's who had lost all of their equipment; blind apparently at the moment they put ashore penniless.

In the confused and gray-scudded dawn of the following day his own crew put down their boat, rowed steadily toward the shore, and there at the grocery store bargained for passage up the beach on the icetruck to the ferry. They would not discuss Cadenhead other than to say that on a clear sea he was a good captain. So saying, lean and ash-gray from their long and steady diet of white navy beans, and still wet and cold from the recent high seas, they climbed into the old icetruck, and without looking out either at the sea and their abandoned white yacht or back at the store where the natives were wishing them well, they rolled up the beach, never to be seen again.

Alone on the yacht, Cadenhead was walking the deck, writing in his log, crawling on his hands and knees, hammering, lashing canvas over the gaping holes, and, like an old crab, dragging material down into the hold. After securing the yacht as best he could, he too put to shore where he asked briefly about the welfare and departure of his crew before inquiring about a temporary lodging for himself.

Thus it was that Cadenhead, late that October, began his daily and unfailing lookout. Each morning he would leave his room at Mrs. Maddy's and go to the beach where over a small driftwood fire he would scramble an egg or cook two slices of bacon. During the morning he would sit sheltered in a tent-half from the biting winds and gaze steadily through the haze or rain at the forlorn yacht. In the afternoons, stirring himself and ranging the length of the beach for planks and boxes washed up from the wreckage of the war-sunk cargo ships and tankers, he would work until dark on the one-room shack that was taking shape between two magnificent dunes, on a flat and bone-strewed gully where once the tornado-driven sea had cut through. Each evening he cooked before his cabin and ate standing, staring out at his distant possession, unheedful of the taunts which were directed at him by the laughing singing fishermen going out or coming in. Wiping the grease from his young wild beard he would stare after them and spit into their fresh tracks.

Occasionally Keppin Devron and Rona came and fished near the completed shack; and sometimes he would join them. Together the three would cast and reel, silently, commenting only when a catch was landed, or more rarely when one escaped.

One night in late winter Keppin Devron, having heard the fresh racking cough that shook Cadenhead's very bones as they fished, brought down a Thermos bottle of steaming rum to the lantern-lit shack. Cadenhead was sitting up on the cot, shrouded in blankets, when Devron, bidden, entered. They poured their drinks and sat opposite each other in the silence which they both were accustomed to. Whether out of a gratitude for the hot grog which burned through his body, warming for the first time that winter his feet and hands, or whether from a degree of loneliness unusual even in a man as solitary as himself, Cadenhead spoke direct with none of the island gift for small talk, insinuation, and weighty casualness of purpose.

"You feel responsible for me?"

"No." Keppin answered, not casually, but as though previously committed to at least one intimate and searching conversation with this stranger who had come ashore so long ago at night. "Not responsible. Interested. Curious you might say. Maybe kinship."

"Kinship hell. I have no kin. Father and a brother but no real kin." He drank from the Thermos cup. "No offense."

"Nope."

"What is it you're curious about? Speak up. I may not talk again."

"Nothing specific." Keppin Devron spoke gravely with a reserve and dignity that would not let him question.

"Good. There's nothing to me. Out yonder is me. That yacht. It's everything I've ever dreamed of, worked, stole, lied, cheated, and married for. There's nothing else." He hugged two blankets about his neck, clutching them desperately with grime-nailed fingers to his chest. His red-webbed eyes were deep in the lamp-shadowed sockets, and his voice was thin when he spoke, softly, as though Keppin Devron were not sitting there respectfully looking away.

"You have a dream. And you know it's a good dream. I worked a long time. Thirty-seven jobs from the day I quit high school till I shipped out at eighteen on an old merchant ship. What a joke that was. Young, full of ambition of a sea career, full of ideals about what a ship should be. Oh I'd read too much. A ship was a universe. It was the perfect escape, the perfect, clean, and man-made world of law and order. And then I saw that first captain, what a sonovabitch he was, and that stinking tub and the filthy, brutal, lying, cheating passel of self-made bastards aboard her. And not just that ship. One wasn't enough to kill such a world as I had in mind; yeah, I was gut-strong in those days. It took a hundred. Yet each time I boarded a new ship, I'd stand in the bow and look at her and see her in my mind's eye as she should be, shipshape and clean, happy, proper, and proud with a fine crew that popped-to and a captain who knew the proper respect for his men and I'd swear to myself to have such a ship. But each voyage was the same. When you see in your mind's eye a ship the way I did, you aren't likely to find her in any ordinary harbor. So I quit the sea till I could buy my own craft. That yacht out there and that with the crew gone. Not one of them realized a boat can be a universe and you can make it what you will."

His cough racked through him and seemed so certainly to be tearing him bodily apart that for a moment Devron leaned forward to catch the blankets which were, in the frenzy, being scattered about.

Cadenhead squeezed his thick rheumy eyes and wiped the cough tears from his gray face and glistening beard. "You'd better go," he said. "Thanks for the drink."

The two men stood up in their usual silence. "One more thing," Cadenhead said while Devron paused in the open door. "Don't repeat what I've said. I may be drunk or delirious. At any rate it's nobody's business. Hear me, old man?"

Devron offered his hand in silent promise before going out onto the night beach where the late winter wind was making snow flurries of the sand.

Each day, shaking and bending double, lassoed by great strangling coughs, Cadenhead, bearded, dirty, and smelling, with his coat sleeve pinned at the shoulder, moved slowly up the gully of whistling cold air to the hard-surface road and to the post office where he anxiously demanded a letter. He never seemed to believe Miss Hannah when she said: "Still nothing." Often he stood on the steps before the open mail window and cussed a round of names. One day in early March, just as he had left the hard-surface, a yellow convertible roared honking down the road. He spun quickly back and half-running, half-limping, as though all the racking cold had settled in his foot, he chased the car to where it was now stopping across from the post office.

The driver, a Cornwallis fisherman, was already out holding open the door when Cadenhead, forehead blue-white and popping sweat beads, arrived. A tremendous frowzy

and rumpled blonde climbed out dragging and tugging at
her thick bright purple coat. She gave a regal flounce to the
white fox collar that settled about her shoulders and across
her heavy bosom. She inspected the heels of one purple
pump and the grease on her bare plump ankle before looking up at Cadenhead who was regarding her in half-amused
wonder.

"Cadenhead!" she screamed in actual astonishment when,
after studying this bearded man, she recognized him. "Cadenhead." She seemed inclined to throw herself into his
arms, then paused, and offered her hand of clinking rings.

The disguise, she chattered hysterically, was perfect and
were the whiskers real and where had he ever found those
vastly amusing clothes and why was he hiding in such a
darling outfit on such a completely isolated place, maybe
from the police, and naturally she had not written but had
simply left Miami which was really dreadfully dull when
she received his forwarded letter but she couldn't believe
the boat would still be afloat. How perfectly droll and
could they leave absolutely at once for Barbados. On she
talked ignoring the staring natives and the restlessness of
Cadenhead's eyes. Finally she screeched again with
laughter, screamed darling, and kissed him above his eyes,
leaving large orange lips gaping lasciviously from his forehead. Cadenhead leaned forward; and while pretending to
study the back seat, where a fur coat was trapped in the
skelter of air luggage, wiped the lips from his forehead, and
then sat down behind the steering wheel. "Get in," he com-
manded.

The blonde was on the island three days, during which
time the islanders were full of talk about the hard drinking,
shouting, and general brawling heard day and night near the
shack. By God she had no money and she could not apparently shout these words loud enough or often enough to

please herself or Cadenhead. No! She would not sell the car and the coat!

On the fourth morning they drove up at the grocery store just as Keppin Devron and Rona were passing toward the beach. "There she is!" the blonde woman screamed. "I've seen you at the shack watching every move Cadenhead makes. Take him. You can have him. If you can get him away from that boat. I can't. Here. Here he is! Take him! He . . ."

But at that second Cadenhead slapped her soft face. The blonde bent over the front fender and laughed and cried with astonishing abandon.

"Who wants a ride up to the ferry?" Cadenhead asked the four men sitting on the bench. At last one shyly volunteered. "Get in," Cadenhead ordered the big blonde. She crawled in behind the wheel and the fisherman crept in and made himself small beside her. The yellow car backed up, swerved through the sand, and disappeared between two dunes.

Keppin Devron stood entranced but Rona was running off in the opposite direction, away from the beach, away from Devron, and away from Cadenhead. She was holding her forehead and was crying. Cadenhead strode to the post office, where he knocked sharply on the unopened window and demanded again the letter which still had not arrived.

All the islanders whispered that Cadenhead was broke; and with the beginning of warm weather he often ranged the hard-surface, and never refused either work or an invitation to eat. When he was not scavenging for work, or fishing with new intent, he would row out to the crippled ship and stay all day, explaining upon return his plans for floating her on one of the first spring full tides. The natives usually waited until he was out of sight before scoffing at a man

so deluded and willfully mad that he could look at a wreck
and expect it to float, could not tell when a ship was lost,
aye, was breaking to pieces in his very face.

Late in April the letter, which he had demanded morning
after morning, arrived. He read it to himself while walking
the windy gully toward the shack. A restlessness seemingly
caught from the brisk and variable spring wind seized him
and carried him rapidly through the grass dunes toward the
pine woods through the cedar stumps and marshes. It was a
crazy dance he was held in, like the hunger-tethered flight
of a sea gull over a shrimp boat. He ranged the beach until
off in the distance he saw Keppin Devron hunched over,
working. When Keppin, glancing up at the wind-cleared
sky, saw him, Cadenhead slowed his pace and approached
in his usual long dignified strides.

"I haven't seen you," Cadenhead paused, out of breath,
and thought, "since my wife left." He thought again. "No.
Not since then."

Keppin returned his attention to the snarled reel. "I've
been going out with the fleet." The two men remained silent
until finally Keppin spoke again: "I didn't know she was
your wife."

"Yes. She was. My second. She's gone to get a divorce
now." Again, as though he had not said it before, he said:
"I haven't seen you about, or Rona."

Keppin glanced quickly up when Rona was mentioned.
Yellow wrinkles cut furrows in his new-brown forehead as
he probed the snarled line. "I reckon not."

Cadenhead studied him awhile longer. Then turning his
back to the whipping wind he spoke quickly. "Got this
today." He unfolded the crumpled letter from his grease-
stained jacket. "The letter I was waiting for. From my
father."

"Yes," Keppin said in a tone that did not admit either curiosity or ignorance.

"Read it. See what you think."

Devron regarded the letter with an obvious respect for its privacy. But then squinting with his humorous blue eyes, he regarded Cadenhead and, not wishing to offend, balanced his words carefully. "I'm busy. But read it aloud if you like."

Cadenhead steadied the paper in the whipping wind and read in a voice which became even deeper and more majestic, apparently in mockery of a voice even more bass than his own:

Dear Shaffer: Whether your monotonous and absurd demands for money are purely for the purpose of outraging and mocking me further, or whether, as you claim, you are in dire threat of losing your boat, I have no way of knowing, and fortunately, as one of the bounties of old age, little energy to care. I know only that I have watched mutely while you exploited and if possible crippled every person who stood between you and the gangplank of that white yacht which would be most certainly, you prophesied, the "perfect craft."

Even this late I find that you are still using criminal methods in your attempts to be a captain. Your last threatening letter had the effect of making me tired, but certainly not afraid; and I have turned it over to my lawyers for whatever legal amusement it may afford them, and for further assurance that you will not be permitted any substantial part of the estate after my eagerly awaited death. I had naturally hoped that you would someday realize that the quest is the important part of the grail, but until you do I cannot refrain from praying that your justly damned boat will sink.

Cadenhead laughed in short explosives. "That was my fifth ace. Not even money enough to sue the coast guard now that I can estimate the full damage."

"What about the ten thousand you had when you signed the contract with that GI outfit?"

"I never had ten thousand. All paper manipulation."
Cadenhead laughed and started off again in the driven
dance. He called back: "Drop by the hut tonight for a
drink." He observed the wonder on Keppin Devron's face.
"The last I had on the boat bar. I've been saving it for this
answer." He hit his chest pocket which held the crumpled
letter and was off again in the crazy dance, now walking,
now running.

That evening, spring moonlight blanched the whalebones
and giant shells and ran like a fire-river through the gully
cut by the wind. Along on his sand dune Cadenhead gazed
out at the stricken yacht and hummed quietly to himself.
He did not seem to know at what moment Keppin first
stood behind him in the silent sand. "The tide runs high,"
Cadenhead said easily.

"It does." Keppin agreed. "Yet the wind has died." He
stretched out on the sand near Cadenhead and looked at the
ragged shadow of the yacht. His hands worked nervously
through the loose sand and around the grass roots, probing,
searching; at the same time his lips were finding and aban-
doning unspoken words. Cadenhead was secretly watching
this agitation, but continued casually with a square of
metal writing his name in the sand, pressing it out, and writing and embellishing it anew, each time more elaborately.

Startled, Keppin discovered the narrow eyes watching
him. His glance darted seaward, moonward, and through
the sand, over the ornate name and elegant hand, up the
rag sleeve to the bearded face and hawk eyes that were
watching him relentlessly. He looked away. Finally his eyes
seized upon the metal in Cadenhead's hand. His voice was
exaggerated in slowness and his words pounded on it pulse-
like. "Do you know what that is?"

Cadenhead, still steady in gaze, held the square of metal
on his open palm. "No, what?"

Devron took it and examined it with excess exactness and interest. "It's part of an old Spanish breastplate." He held it over his pectoral muscle.

"How did you know?" Cadenhead continued to study the troubled man.

"The old galleon's buried over there. We used to dig hereabouts for coins and spikes and bits of armor when I was a boy."

"Where?" Cadenhead pushed himself to his feet and stumbled uncertainly in the direction Keppin had pointed. "Where? I've never seen a wreckage near."

"Hereabouts. Maybe the sand's covered it completely now." Devron's voice was relaxing slowly. "Part of the prow used to stick straight skyward when I was a boy. We used to play 'pirate' there."

"Real Spanish coins?"

"Not many. Not gold. One or two. But thousands of bits of iron: hinges and the like."

"Maybe it was a treasure ship."

"No, not likely. The gold ships seldom ventured this far north. And Kidd and the pirates were down between here and Sea Island. There's treasure on down. Here though. . . ." He kicked the sand. "Just a ship." They walked through the tall grass, kicking the sand—until, stopping, Devron waved his arm overhead in a childish flourish. "Here." He pointed to a double row of iron spikes which outlined a boat prow against a low sandhill. "The sea was there." He pointed to the steep dunes which hid the ocean and the new beach. "The beach is building up here. Fast too. I'll probably live to see it reach Star Point."

"A ship. Here." Cadenhead mumbled, unaware of being heard. "Buried." He stumbled drunkenly back to his dune where the bottle of rye was stuck like a jib boom in the sand. He drank and coughed and wiped his matted beard with the sleeve of his filthy jacket. He offered the remaining few drops to Devron who refused. "I thought you came out for a drink." Cadenhead's eyes burned with reflected moonlight.

Devron slapped his fist with the open palm of his other hand. "I came down to talk."

Letting himself down gently onto the soft sand dune Cadenhead asked: "About what?"

Devron crouched on his knees and again nervously sifted sand through his frightened fingers. "Rona."

"Ah." Cadenhead grinned, knowingly, wickedly.

"And what your wife said at the store."

Cadenhead's grin widened from wickedness to lewd delight. "Oh."

"What did she mean?" The slow casualness was gone from Devron's voice.

"I don't remember what she said." Cadenhead shrugged his shoulders in a gesture of ignorance.

Devron crouched, tense, his words rapid and impersonal. "About you and Rona."

"That?" Cadenhead laughed. "I don't know."

Devron stood up and glared down at the man. "You do."

Cadenhead arched an eyebrow, dead quiet, then observing better Devron's scowl answered: "I hadn't thought of it. Why did she say that about Rona? Maybe because that's the way she feels about men and she can't imagine a woman feeling any other way."

Devron's fists unclinched. Cadenhead rose uneasily to his feet and weaved as he walked toward the sea. "Or maybe she discovered the truth."

"You mean you think Rona's in love with you."

"Damned if I know. What does she say?"

"She doesn't say anything. She won't talk about you or about that day or about that woman. Fact is: she doesn't seem to want to talk to me about anything any more." Like a fringe of grass fire the white waves were eating at the beach. The two men trod the hard-packed sand, gazing oceanward at the jagged shadow of the yacht through the thickening air. "Even her folks say she's strange now and odd-like. And naturally everybody talks about what was said and how we aren't seen much together any more."

"They do?" Cadenhead was smiling with immense pleasure.

"Mr. Bruton wants her to go down and visit her brothers in New Orleans."

"Brothers? I thought she was the only child."

"There's Rona and then there are the twins: Cawdor and Thane."

Cadenhead snapped his fingers and whirled rapidly. "They're the boys with the fleet of tugs and river barges!" He slapped his hand against his flanks like a young crowing gamecock.

"I'll be damned. I knew that. Why didn't I remember? I heard about them before I got that company from Norfolk. And then I forgot. They were too far away. I'll be damned. They're her *brothers?*" He giggled aloud to himself. "How old is Rona?" If he had been more sober and less full of this intense jubilance, he might have seen all the humor and gentleness and every trace of friendship leave Keppin Devron's face. Instead he was squinting his eyes to cut through the moonlit fog which was covering the white yacht.

"How old?" he repeated as though the answer had been given and he had not heard.

"Eighteen."

Cadenhead's laugh muffled the whisper of Devron's steps as he disappeared down the tornado gully.

Flowing over the beach and through the gully the warm fog lake spilled over the rusty red roof of the shack and over the swaying grass on the dunes. Cadenhead cackled and kicked sandspray and danced a drunken hornpipe. He grasped the soft fog by the hips and followed up the gully in a wild conga, out of the seafog, onto the road, and down to the store where in the light of the gas pumps two men were playing checkers on the carved squares of the bench between them.

"Oh where and oh where does my bonnie lassie live?" He sang in a deep merry voice and shuffle-danced, grinning at the two men. "Where's Rona live?"

"On down near Baxter. The big yellow house."

"Oho!" Cadenhead saluted a toy-soldier salute, bowed, and was off down the road singing: "Come out come out wherever you are!"

He did not turn back to see Keppin Devron come out from the store and pump three gallons of gasoline into a jerry-can which he carried into the fog toward the yacht.

Long after midnight a jeepload of youngsters swerved to a stop on the hard-surface four miles beyond Baxter. Cadenhead was sitting in the middle of the road. He accepted without thanks the ride offered him on the hot hood of the Birddog. He was mumbling to himself: "She wouldn't even talk to me. Wouldn't even open the door. 'Go away,' they said. Like a drunk tramp. Me." Back at the store, now dark, the Birddog bounced off the highway and plowed through the sand ruts down toward the shack. Gaining the hard beach sand it raced along the water-edge and was turning sharply around when Cadenhead stood up and was thrown over the hood and onto the hard-packed sand.

He jumped to his feet and ran limping to the land's edge. Out off Star Point a light was blazing: the yacht was burning. "Hurry. Get help!" he yelled to the kids as he ran limping to his boat. "Hurry." He pushed off into the cove. "Dammit. Hurry," he screamed as the Birddog plowed past.

All night the ship burned. The coast guard worked dangerously close to save her, then fell back exhausted. The fishermen on their way out and the night fleet on its way in detoured to watch as the yacht, listing more precariously, waved fire-flags at the distant shore which in the early dawn was crawling with people. Cadenhead, driven back by the coast guard, circled madly in his boat shouting for help above the crackle and hiss of the fork-tongued flames. Once he eluded the guard and rowed straight in but was pushed back by the white heat. Finally, when he could row and shout no more, he sat open-mouthed and stupid with exhaustion. The coast guard men again threw him a line which this time he accepted. With swollen fingers Cadenhead, entranced, secured the line and sat watching the leaping flames that still gorged on the ship. As the coast guard boat towed him slowly away, the white yacht wallowed over, hissed live steam, blew white smoke, and dived under the burning oil-slick.

Cadenhead walked through the natives who gathered round and followed in his wake, like waves from the bow. Shoulders sagging, he limped to the cabin and in the half-dark stared with smoke-reddened eyes about him. He kicked over the canvas cot and opened a secret door in the baseboard. From there he pulled out the leather case with the ship's silver. He unfastened it, dreamily touched the purple velvet and the silver, then shut the lid. Glaring about him, he painfully reached to a rafter for an immaculate white- and gold-braided captain's cap. Pulling it low over his smoke-blackened, blistered, and greasy face, he stumbled out of the shack.

He was coughing and wheezing with desperation as he shuffled up the gully, ignoring the sympathies of the natives who were all saying: "It happened so fast." He sat on the checkerboard bench, wheezing painfully, and staring dumbly. "Cigarette?" he finally managed to beg in a hoarse whisper. He lit one, took a long draw, exhaled, and gasping again for air, he dropped the cigarette and pocketed the pack.

When the ferry-bound icetruck pulled off the highway, Cadenhead climbed in, Mrs. Maddy handed the driver a dollar and another to Cadenhead who, without looking down at the natives or into the store where Rona was numbly sitting or at the side of the store where Keppin Devron stood with bandaged hands and blistered wrists, signaled the iceman to drive on. The old icetruck rumbled up to the end of the highway and out between the sand dunes and on up the beach through the screeching laughter of the seagulls and the maniacal applause of the surf.

BIG GOAT,
LITTLE GOAT

There was a friendliness about my Uncle Jim that attracted children to him, and it was this friendliness, I thought, that set him apart from my other uncles and made him different. When they spoke harshly to him, I imagined it was through jealousy, and then I would want to whisper my explanation, as though I were his uncle and he my nephew. That day Uncle Harry had just shouted at him: "I'm not going to buy you a goat. So quit talking about it."

"Don't pay any attention to him," I said.

"I don't," Uncle Jim answered, putting his arm on my shoulder—for at ten I was as tall as he. We walked together to his shop in the back yard, and in a few minutes he was laughing again, showing me his saws, his hammers, his homemade kites and an openmouthed, glass-eyed skunk that was stuffed and mounted on a limb.

His shop was the old greenhouse where my great-aunt

had once raised sweet peas and ferns for a funeral home. Three sides of the shop were of glass panes, the fourth was the brick wall of Grandmother's kitchen. The floor, of hard-packed dirt, was about four feet lower than the ground outside. My uncle, by leaning against the window sill, could watch through the glass the black ants commuting from their sand hills to a dead beetle or a cake crumb. Sometimes, when the ants were not working, he stared at the tall grass that grew almost on the level with his eyes. Or again, on rainy afternoons, he leaned back against the kitchen wall and watched the patterns the trickling water made on the panes, as drop joined drop, hanging for a moment, then sliding uncertainly to the sill. At times, long after dusk, he sat looking at I don't know what while my aunts and other uncles called vainly to him from the kitchen window. You have seen people who because they are warm again after being cold cannot move from an armchair before an open fire; that is the way my uncle was after he had been watching the ants working and the grass blades fencing.

That morning, after showing me all the things I had seen many times before, he opened the big wardrobe cabinet Aunt Nan had used to keep vases in. The shelves of the cabinet were lined now with Mason jars full of pecans. He took down a row of jars and placed them in a neat line on the table. Methodically, he opened each jar and put the top in front of it. And then, with little finger extended, he carefully picked a pecan, handling it as though it were a robin's egg, and placed it in the top he'd just unscrewed from the jar. During this ritual his expression was intense, his white eyebrows twitched, and once he muttered—either to himself or the pecans, I didn't know which.

All of this completed, he stepped back and waited for my approval. When I stood without saying anything, he smiled and said, "They're all different sizes." He touched each jar separately with his thin fingers. "These and these and these. All different sizes. These and these and these." He went on touching jars.

"How about these?"

"Yes. These too. And these and these and these and these." He had a way of saying a word so many times it didn't seem like the same word, or any word at all—but as though it were a sound that had a meaning only for himself and sometimes me. That day, saying "these," he filled the workshop with a drone as though a hundred tiny bees were swarming about our heads and in our ears. To keep from being dizzy I studied the pecans so carefully that I saw the magic he had done with them: there must have been fifty jars there, and each one held nuts of a different size. Between the largest pecan and the smallest anyone could tell the difference, but between the largest and the next-to-the-largest only Uncle Jim could distinguish. He tried to teach me but he couldn't.

"Hold out both hands," he said. He placed a pecan in each palm and closed my fingers over them. "Now which is bigger?"

"This one," I said, extending the left hand. He took them back, balanced them carefully in his wrinkled palms, shut his eyes and whispered again to himself or the pecans, "No. This one."

I tried with more, but always the one in the left hand felt bigger. "Shut your eyes," he said. "That's the way to tell."

When I missed again Uncle Jim was disgusted, or tried to be. "Look. I can tell this way." He picked up two pecans and held them behind his back. "This one is bigger."

We went out to the end of the yard, looked at the bare pecan trees and raked around in the dead leaves for more nuts, but he had got them all two months before. During those months he had sat in the greenhouse and sorted them from the crocus sacks into the Mason jars. "You've *got* to learn," he said as we walked back to the shop. He seemed so earnest that I felt ashamed of my dullness. He lit the small round oil heater, pulled the last sack of pecans from under the work table and sat down to sort them.

"You teach me how," I said, "and I'll teach you how to tell time." The nearest Uncle Jim could come to telling the exact time was by saying, "It's almost three," or, "It's way after four." He could read the little hand but the long hand puzzled him. While we worked I tried to explain that when the long hand pointed to "one" it meant "five." He shut his eyes as though he were holding the "one" in his left palm and the "five" in his right, and then he said, "Later. I'll learn later."

"Why not now?"

"Because it's the same time every day. This is different, though." He placed another pecan in a jar.

"What do you do with them when you get a jar full?"

"Nan uses them in the kitchen. She puts them in cakes and things."

"Well, why then do you have to separate them like this?"

Uncle Jim looked up reproachfully. "You got to learn what's big and what's little. That's something you got to learn."

"After lunch. Are we going to work after lunch?"

"No. I'm going to take you to see the little black goat I told you about." He frowned, thinking I suppose of Uncle Harry's harsh words. "I don't see why everybody don't like goats."

During lunch Uncle Jim didn't mention the goat. He didn't talk at all except once when he whispered, "Hurry up." We went back out to the shop to get a kite to fly and a pocketful of unsorted pecans to eat. We walked down through the grove and out the back gate, down Farrell Street and past Clancey's grocery store.

Across from the grocery store was a big field where the city had begun construction on a concrete stadium when the Depression began. Tall grass had grown up now and stood brown and silver over the field. Narrow paths cut through it with a directness and timesaving simplicity that paved walks seem never to have.

My uncle chose the narrowest of these, no wider than a plank, and we followed it to where a clump of cottonwood trees had grown up among the concrete pillars which were to have supported the bleachers. Before we reached the trees, we heard the goat baa. Uncle Jim stopped and held his arms out slightly, like a rooster cooling himself, as a motion for me behind him to halt.

Instead of quickening his pace, though, he walked slower when he moved again. We bent and crept under the cottonwood. On the other side, near the center of a bare circle, the black goat danced. His rope was wound round and round the iron pipe in the center as though he had in a secret ritual been trotting deliberately around the circle. Now when he jumped up and kicked, the rope was so short that it jerked him to the ground.

"Sammy," Uncle Jim said. He'd never mentioned before that the goat had a name. Sammy quit dancing and pressed his short nubby horns against my uncle's knees. Uncle Jim unwound the rope and then took the goat by the horns. He pushed and the goat pushed; he laughed and the goat bleated.

"Play with him!" Uncle Jim said generously when he was out of breath.

"He stinks," I said, looking at the matted black hair thick and lumpy with burrs and hanging with dead leaves and straw. "He stinks."

"Not if you don't smell him," Uncle Jim said; but still I could not share his enthusiasm. Uncle Jim looked hurt when I started fastening the cord on the kite.

"Over there's where you run. Go down toward the collard patch in that clearing and run this way. Let 'er have all the string you got." The wind was strong and steady and the kite, flat against the breeze, dived and darted for a minute, then found its course and rose steadily up and out against the gray winter sky. While I played out the string my uncle talked to the goat. Then he came over to me, flushed and out of breath. "He was glad to see me."

"Yeah," I said.

"I'm going to buy him."

"Yeah."

"Yes."

"How? Who're you gonna buy him from?"

"Potter. He's the colored man who owns him. He's the one who raises those collards. Only they're dead now. The police didn't know he was raising collards out here. They don't even know Sammy lives out here in the daytime."

"You've got no money."

"He just wants a dollar and a quarter for him."

"Have you got that much?"

"I will have. I've already got this much." He stretched open the pocket of his thick coat sweater, pulled out a handkerchief and unknotted the corner where the change was tied. He had thirty-five cents in pennies and nickels.

"That's not enough."

"Almost, though."

"No, it's not."

"Yes, it is," he said, shaking the coins in his cupped hands. "Listen."

"You need twice that much. Even more than that."

"I'll get it. By-and-by," he said.

"Where'd you get that?"

"Nan. She gives me money when she takes a jar of my pecans. I'll get the rest."

"From Aunt Nan?"

Uncle Jim looked over toward Clancey's grocery store. I couldn't tell whether he was wishing or remembering when he began speaking: "I'm going to work for him."

"Does he know it?"

Uncle Jim wasn't listening. "Yesterday I went in there to see him about it. He's talking to this old gypsy lady. She wants some birdseed and Clancey doesn't want her to have birdseed 'cause he sells birdseed to Mrs. Jacobs for her yellow bird. Clancey he acts like he doesn't see me. He does, though." Uncle Jim stopped for breath. "He sees me. 'Clancey,' I said, 'you give this poor old gypsy all the birdseed she wants. Her little bird is starving to death.' "

"What did Clancey say?"

"He laughed. 'Jim,' he said, 'she doesn't want any birdseed. This is cornstarch.' And she ups and says, 'I ain't no gypsy either!' "

"What did you say?"

"I said, 'Well, why you want to look so much like a gypsy then?' And Clancey says, 'Jim, you watch out how you talk to her,' and so I hit him in the stomach."

"You didn't, Uncle Jim!"

"Yes, I did. Her too."

"Aw, Uncle Jim, you did not!"

"No," he said, "but I thought about it. I wish now I had."

"But did you ask him about the job?"

"No."

"Well then, let's go over there now."

"All right. Let's go," Uncle Jim said. But when we started pulling the kite in he said, "Maybe we ought to wait till tomorrow."

"I'll be gone home tomorrow."

"That's right." He thought for a long time. "I'll tell you. You just don't go home tomorrow. You just stay here and help me get the goat."

"I got to go. I'll help you today. Maybe you can take him

home tonight." Uncle Jim tried to keep from looking happy. He ran back to where the goat was standing, staring at him and chewing. The kite relaxed and settled on a thorny locust bush a few yards away. While I untangled the cord, Uncle Jim talked to the goat. He got down on his hands and knees and pressed his forehead against the goat's horns. They eyed each other and rolled their heads from side to side.

Uncle Jim didn't say anything as we walked across the field toward the store. Through the window we could see Clancey weighing corn meal into ten-cent packages.

"Come on, let's go ask him."

"No," Uncle Jim said. "I asked him."

"What did he say?"

"He said 'No.' "

"Why?"

Uncle Jim's lips moved and he frowned as though the light were too bright—the way he always did when I asked him why he didn't have an office, a car, a wife and children of his own. "Come on. Let's go home," he said. "I'll show you the pecans."

As we walked up Farrell Street against the wind, I said, "He smelled bad, anyway."

"He was sure glad to see me, though," my uncle said. "He don't jump that way for Potter or anybody else but me."

"Thirty-five cents," I said. "Maybe Aunt Nan'll buy a lot of pecans at once."

"No. Always just enough for church money and one week. That's what she always says."

"If you told her you were going to buy a goat. Maybe."

"I'm not going to tell her. I'm going to surprise her. One of these days she's going to be in the kitchen and she's going to say, 'Why, I believe to my heart I hear a kitten mewing.

Why, no, I believe it's a baby crying right out there in your workshop, Jim!' And she'll go out and there Sammy'll be, standing under the table where it's good and warm." The way he talked about the animal made my throat tighten up like when you fall out of a tree and don't want anybody to know you're hurt.

"If she won't buy them, maybe Clancey will," I said as we turned in the back gate.

"Reckon?"

"I don't know. You wanna try?"

"If you want to," he said.

He chose the jars carefully, lining them up on the table as he had done before. One after another he put them back again. "No, I can't let him have these. Or these." He would have put them all back if I hadn't reminded him that today was the last day I could help him. Finally, after an almost endless amount of exchanging, he selected eleven jars. He carried six, pressing them against his chest with his arms, and I carried five. "We may have to come back if this isn't enough," I said.

No one saw us as we went back out the gate and down the street. At the store we kicked against the screen and Clancey came from behind the long counter to let us in. "Well, well, well," he said. "What've you got here, Mr. Jim? This your son? You didn't tell me you were still running around with that blonde, Mr. Jim." Clancey winked at me. "And where's the lady now?"

I waited for Uncle Jim to speak, but he was quiet the way he was at the table or whenever any grown person was around. "Do you want to buy some pecans?" I said. We talked about them for a while. I told him they belonged to Uncle Jim and that it was all right for us to sell them. Uncle Jim stood silently in front of a big wicker basket of country eggs. While we talked he picked up two and held one in each hand, weighing each in his own mind. But he was listening to every word at the same time.

"Ten cents a pound and that won't leave me much of a profit. What you going to do with all this money, Mr. Jim? Get drunk?"

Uncle Jim turned red and gripped the eggs in his fist. Clancey popped open a sixteen-pound paper bag and put it on the scales. He opened the first jar and poured it into the sack and then, before we could say anything, the second one.

"No! Don't do that!" Uncle Jim cried.

"What's that, Mr. Jim?" Clancey laughed as he opened the third jar.

"Don't mix them. They're all separated."

"Now, Mr. Jim. They're mine now, so you just let me do with them like I want." He was still laughing as he poured the third jar in. He was looking at the pointer on the scales and reaching for the fourth jar when my uncle threw the egg at him. It hit on top of the scales and splattered in the groceryman's face. Before I could get to him my uncle threw the other egg, but it missed.

"You fool. You goddam fool," Clancey yelled. He started around the counter, but Uncle Jim was already at the door. I ran after him up the street and Clancey stood in front of the grocery store, hollering at us until we were out of sight. It had all happened so fast that I didn't even stop to think that I should explain to Clancey how hard my uncle had worked sorting the nuts. All I knew was that Clancey was screaming, "I'm going to call the police."

We stopped in the back yard to see if he was following us. Then Uncle Jim ran for the shop. He tried to shut the door before I could get in. We were both breathing hard, and my uncle was trembling all over. He leaned back against the brick wall and said between breaths, "Help hide me." He sank to the floor and began crawling under the table. "See if he's coming," he said. I peeped out the window and when I turned back around Uncle Jim had covered himself with crocus sacks so that only his head and feet showed under the dark table. I moved the last sack of pecans so that his head could not be seen from the door and put a dead fern in front of his feet. Even under the sacks he trembled as though he were freezing to death. "Do you want the heater lit?" I asked.

"No," he said.

"You want me to hide under there with you?"

"No."

"You want the skunk under there with you?" I asked.

He was sobbing now and didn't answer, so I put the stuffed skunk down behind the bag where he could reach it if he wanted to. I opened the door of the greenhouse and started out to find a place where I could be by myself. As I went up the steps I heard my uncle say, as though it were a childhood nursery rhyme, "They're going to lock me up."

Several times since then I have heard persons in moments of deep concern utter words that seemed to come from the very center of their being and of their loneliness. My uncle's words that winter afternoon had such a sound, and I did not know whether to go back into the greenhouse or out into the open. I stood on the steps, waiting and listening. A gray squirrel dropped with a noise like a bullet to the tin roof of the greenhouse, and in a rhythm like a pounding pulse raced across the narrow open space and jumped into silence on the other side.

THE WANTON
TROOPERS

The wanton troopers riding by
Have shot my fawn, and it will die.

—ANDREW MARVELL

Between the Café Mona and Saint-Germain-des-Près, in the heart of the Latin Quarter, the Académie André is hidden in a mossy courtyard behind huge and peeling dark-green doors which open onto a tiny crippled street, which itself is almost hidden from the stranger who passes on the big boulevard or on the rue de Rennes.

Here in the Académie, in the early 1950's, half the students were American, half were French. The Americans, for the most part, were World War II veterans who reported to class as though to work, put in their hours, and at the end of the month drew their subsistence checks on the G.I. Bill which permitted veterans to study in certain schools abroad. The French were not so regimentalized and industrious. They wandered in and out and the only ones who appeared regularly and stayed the entire day were the young girls who were inscribed here by their bourgeois parents in an effort to keep them out of the existentialists' bars and cafés on the Place St. Germain.

Sitting in the vestibule, peeling potatoes for her *pot-au-feu* or making innumerable checked aprons for her little grandson who played all day in the cold courtyard or upstairs where some heat drifted through from the ateliers, Madame Hélène watched these girls with rational, penetrating eyes, just as she watched everything that transpired in the three huge studios of the Académie. She was a short, rather pudgy-looking woman of about fifty, and it was only when one saw her tiptoeing into a still-life class hugging a heavy granite bust of Victor Hugo that one realized her quiet and powerful strength.

There was a rumor that fifteen years ago she had dragged a male model, a well-known Olympic athlete, out of the atelier, through the vestibule, and wrestled him across the courtyard before pushing him naked into the street. Madame Hélène herself was always exasperated when asked about the incident. She would throw her short arms toward heaven and explain in rapid French that indeed it did not happen thus. The man was posing in an old studio where the office now is and after an argument about his fees she merely pushed him down the stairs, after which it was an easy matter to kick him into the courtyard, where he was allowed to dress. For certainly she had more respect and sentiment for the dignity of the Académie than to throw such a man into the street. After all, she would conclude, was it not she who preserved the decorum of the school? Was it not she (and then she would go off into a terrible argot which the Americans could not understand but which the French students would explain with wicked delight) who prevented orgies, of such total degradation that even

Chicago would be shocked, from taking place in the ateliers
and here in the vestibule and there on the stairs? She would
grow voluble and specific and point to the courtyard and
to various shrieking, protesting students while describing
the horrible, intense debauchery which she alone, she,
Madame Hélène, for twenty-two years had prevented from
being enacted here in this sacred Académie where Claude
Félix Cambronne had studied and painted.

Listening to her without understanding her words, it was
impossible to know whether Madame Hélène believed
them or whether she merely raved for the entertainment of
the French students and the bewilderment of the Americans.
In any case, it was true that she could, without seeming to
glance up from her potatoes, detect a flirtation and she
often recognized the looks of love long before the persons
concerned were aware of their own involvement.

For several months last winter she regarded with attentive, impartial eye the coy behavior of Anna Barkova
toward Nebraska Long. Nebraska was actually born in
Iowa and his strong Midwestern accent had a slight Swed-
ish lilt which rendered it less painful, even amusing, to
Madame Hélène. But then Nebraska had early and accidentally tendered himself sweet to that woman by appearing impressed to learn that Claude Félix Cambronne had
studied and painted in this very Académie. (At that time
Nebraska, seated always mentally at the far end of the table
from his august and chauvinistic landlady, was morbidly
ashamed of his education, so that he dared not ask deferen-
tially as the Americans usually did, or boldly as the French,
just who exactly was this Claude Félix Cambronne.) Later,
after Christmas, when Madame Hélène took him upstairs
to her one-room living quarters and showed him a little oil
study, twelve by eighteen, that Cambronne had done of
her some thirty years before when she was a young girl with

a plain but truly rapturous and innocent visage, he had had
the presence to say that it was certainly a nice thing; and
then he had had the gallantry to say that he found her face
more interesting now. That was, she said, indeed too
charming of him. He had gazed closely at the portrait again
and when he looked up at her aging face in the slanted
light, they both had turned suddenly, unexpectedly red. She
had opened the door and apologized for having taken up so
much of his two-hour lunch time.

Nebraska had gone quietly down the steps, across the
courtyard and up the narrow street to Saint-Germain where
he boarded with an old family of women which had lived
there when Saint-Germain was the fashionable *faubourg*
described by Proust. Now two wars, a dead husband, and
three dead sons and two dead grandsons later, Madame
had taken in this young man who wished so much, she explained his presence to visitors, to have the opportunity to
live like a Frenchman, if only for a year. At the long mahogany table, where he often remembered the scrubbed-
board kitchen table in Iowa and the muslin curtains, they
talked lightly of politics, literature, and the ballet. That is
to say, they talked of de Gaulle, Gide (Sartre did not yet
exist for them), and of Serge Lifar. When Nebraska mentioned Melville or any American writer or artist, Madame
la Générale would lift her white eyebrows and demand
whom with such a brilliant and icy smile that Nebraska was
never sure whether it was his pronunciation or his taste
which was being questioned. At such moments, by narrow-
ing his eyes imperceptibly, he could make the candlelight
seem to hesitate, and in the gloom at the far end of the
table the black velvet choker-band about her neck would
blend into the dark draperies behind her and Madame
would be sitting with her head apparently severed completely from her body, guillotined by her own elegance.

He sometimes dreaded these lunches but he remained

here, he told himself, because he liked his tremendous room
with the heavy dark-red velvet hangings, the massive wal-
nut furniture reflected in enormous, gilt-framed mirrors,
and the lustrous parquet floor which squeaked so much like
a well-chain. Here he stayed alone as much as possible and
read American magazines and newspapers bought at Bren-
tano's on his book allowance. Each night he ate out, went
afterward to the nearest concert, and stopped at the Café
Mona to drink a cup of hot milk while listening without
speaking to the difficult and often disagreeable Americans
who drank there every night. A little after midnight he returned home to wash out his nylon shirt and shorts and
once a week his blue jeans.

It was a solitary life but one toward which all during the
army he had planned and saved. "The Solitary Swede,"
they had called him in the army and again in the university,
for he was by nature self-sufficient, happier when not having to think about other people.

The fact that his notebook and pads were full of sketches
of Anna Barkova did not, therefore, mean that he had been
thinking about her that winter. It was simply that he liked
her odd assortment of features and found them so easy to
reproduce that, left free, his hand was apt to trace automatically the dramatic sweep of her hair caught up in back,
her querulous brows and short tilted nose, or her vulnerable, pouting baby mouth with its even row of white baby
teeth. In all, it was the soft, round face of a pampered baby
—except for the eyes which were tremendously large and
dark and, even when she laughed, capable of sorrow. It
was these startling, haunting eyes that confronted one from
every page of Nebraska's sketchboard. Madame Hélène had,
of course, become alert when she first, accidentally, saw
these sketches, and when Anna heard of them she became
immediately fascinated.

When she finally confirmed, by the plain tactic of snatching his notebook from him, that it was true that the bony, balding Midwesterner was using her as a constant model, little Anna approached him each morning after that with a fondness and directness usually put aside for more subtle means by little girls after the age of four. She had absolutely none of the chic and poise one has been taught to expect of young ladies in Paris, and at almost twenty she was still involved in the baby fat that most young people have resolved at ten or twelve.

Even when not interested in attracting anyone's attention her actions were likely to be awkward with the outgrown spontaneity and enthusiasm of a child. During the fall term she had hung like a puppy at the heels of Bernard Lévy and Suzanne as though it never occurred to her that that couple would want sometime to be alone. She never seemed to notice that they were never as overjoyed as she when she had sixty francs with which to buy the three of them coffee. Nebraska could not understand why she should want to buy coffee for a person as physically dirty, uncombed, and rude as Bernard Lévy who shouted continually at the models and at anyone who even accidentally touched him. He never shouted at Anna though and seemed to tolerate her and her extravagant emotions better than anyone else.

When suddenly Anna turned this childish attentiveness on him, Nebraska was abashed, for at thirty he was still shy and wary of women, even the most gentle. He hurried through the vestibule now and took up each day a place between the model and the stove so that Anna could not sit beside him as she had done for several days after snatching his notebook. When he heard her from time to time tiptoeing playfully up behind him and peeping over his shoulder, he held his notebook unintentionally closer to himself.

During the breaks between poses he rushed out into the narrow street where he smoked, and read and reread the stone plaque attached to the building across from the Académie:

Ici Est Tombé
Mort pour La France
Gaston Raoult
Étudiant   Âge 20 ans

At this distance he could not read the engraved date on which the young student had died, and, even though he intended to, he never crossed over to see if the student had fallen, as most of them had according to the plaques scattered all over the city, during the fighting the August of the Liberation.

Soon Anna, watched by Madame Hélène, began following him here to the street before the green doors. Becoming bold, apparently in the belief that he had come here to be followed, she playfully asked him for cigarettes (which later he saw her giving to Suzanne and to the filthy Bernard Lévy). Or she teased him by asking why he did not chew chewing gum like all Americans. He had told her it was because he was fifty-two years old and had false teeth. Even though he had said this to impress upon her the difference in their ages, this was just the sort of nonsense Anna loved and so each day she would try to provoke him out of his silence. One day she said, more seriously: "Do you have a car?"

"Here in Paris?" he asked.

"Anywhere," she said gravely.

"At home," he said.

"A big car?"

"A Plymouth." He was amused by her seriousness on the subject.

"Is that a big car?"

He shrugged his shoulders in the new way. "Medium."
The next day she said: "Do you have a picture of it?"
"What?" he asked.
"Your car, stupid," she said.
"I don't think so." He grinned. "Why?"
She was embarrassed but persisted, now as though it
were a joke: "Search for one."

He had laughed at her but that night he got out his foot-
locker and looked through his photographs. There was one
of the farm taken from the silo, one of the clapboard frame
house, one of his father standing awkwardly in his Sunday
suit down at the dusty road by the heat-blistered, peeling
mailbox, one taken during the war of his mother in over-
alls and his Aunt Hilda in an apron, plucking chickens for
the Saturday market in Watertown, one of himself on the
new tractor, and several of the family and the new tractor,
but none of the car.

"Well then," Anna said when he told her, "you must
draw me a picture of it."

Nebraska's first drawings had been of cars and planes
and his first solution to the problem of foreshortening had
been made one Sunday afternoon sitting by the mailbox
trying to draw a car rounding the curve from Watertown.
Somewhat ashamed, but secretly delighted, and more for
his own pleasure than for hers, he began designing ridiculously elongated, low, streamlined automobiles. When he,
as though by chance, let her see the folio which held them,
he was disappointed in her reaction.

"What is it?" she asked as though greatly annoyed by
the first one.

"My car."

"Stupid," she said. "Nobody has a car that looks like
that." She flipped the pages and looked at the fantastic cars.
"No."

"You don't like them."

"No, no, no. I want you to do a real car. Like you have at home." But she would keep these sketches until he did a sensible one.

That evening, using a big sheet of paper, he drew a caricature of a decrepit T-model bouncing down a bumpy road, the rubbery wheels and axles buckling under it and throwing the driver, in a duster and goggles, a foot off the seat where the springs were crashing through the split cushions. She had laughed when he showed it to her but again she had protested and asked for a picture of his car, the Plymouth, a real picture. In the meantime she would keep the caricature if she might.

The next morning the first truly spring sun was shining, so instead of going to the Académie, Nebraska went down to sketch-in a water color of the little green grocery shop at the corner by Saint-Julien-le-Pauvre. After lunch he went over to the Académie earlier than usual and while taking off his raincoat in the vestibule he could see Anna, Suzanne, and Bernard Lévy sitting on the edge of the model-stand regarding his automobile sketches which were spread out on the floor. Several other French students were standing nearby looking and laughing.

Feeling rather proud that they were amused by his drawings, Nebraska stood at the threshold of the open door ready to enter when he realized they were not laughing at the humor in his designs but rather at Bernard Lévy who was delivering a lecture: ". . . *voilà l'art américain.*"

It was too late for Nebraska to turn back. He entered the studio and walked along the side, back of the model-stand, to his shelf. The laughter ebbed away but Bernard, whether he had seen Nebraska or not, continued his mock lecture. "You will note the texture of the paper. Only the

finest Italian paper for such artists. Naturally. And the
pencil strokes. You will note that they were made with the
finest pencils from Philadelphia. All bought by a government which can purchase anything, produce anything, including art."

Pretending that he did not understand the words—and
all the students assumed that the Americans could understand only simple sentences spoken to them slowly and directly—Nebraska took down a set of water colors and some
brushes and went quietly through the still-life room and
back out into the courtyard. There his calmness left him
and he began shaking all over. He should go back in and
smash the boy in the face and kick the living hell out of
him. Tear up the drawings. Confront Anna with her deceit.

All afternoon he was too furious to work. He walked
along the Seine hating the sight even of it and of the bridges
he usually loved to look at. He would never understand the
French. Not if he lived here forever. Santayana had said
that he had not a single friendship with a Frenchman which
he did not feel was marred by insincerity. Nebraska felt
that they were probably sincere at any given moment but
that they were completely the victims of their varying im-
pulses. They had developed their elaborate rituals of politeness to hide this weakness. Anyway, one could not ac-
cuse Bernard Lévy of being insincere, polished, politic. He
was openly hostile to the Americans. He never spoke to
them. Within their hearing, though, he accused them of
being the new Germans, the new fascists, the new super-
men, the lovers and rebuilders of a Germany that would
again run riot over Europe. Usually, however, when he
glared at them from his corner of the room or at their work,
he was either silent or spoke in argot to the amusement of
the other French. His chief argument against them seemed

to be always that they had the best of supplies, five thousand francs' worth a month, paid for by their government, while he, though he did not mention it, often drew with a black crayon on flattened pages of *Le Monde* which, unlike the other newspapers, had few photographs to interfere with his compositions.

"But it's not fair," Nebraska thought. "There's not an American there who wouldn't give him papers and pencils and brushes. If he weren't too damned proud to accept them." It was true: almost any one of the veterans was pleased when he could find a tactful way to let one of the more talented of the French students have supplies on his bill, if not as an outright gift then in trade for a small composition.

All of the Americans wanted especially to own at least one of the journals on which, using a bamboo stick dipped in India ink, Bernard drew literally hundreds of hollow-eyed, skull faces with gaunt bodies. Sometimes these strange birdlike figures were naked and their ribs and hipbones and thighs were depicted with the terrible accuracy of an anatomical chart. Sometimes they wore hanging, gauzelike clothes and carried shovels that seemed to be as heavy for them as railroad ties. Whether clothed or naked, the stooped bodies were charged with hunger and despair and hopelessness. He worked with a maddening intensity and for weeks he would never look at the model, at whom he nevertheless shouted abuse, but would stand in the back of the room working as though he had a hundred years of work to do in one, drawing and redrawing these haunted, nightmare, wraithlike creatures. At other times but with the same furious intensity, he would draw on gray paper quite marvelous gulls in graceful, lyrical flight. As much as Nebraska, at the moment, despised the boy, he would have given without hesitation his next month's supply allowance for one page of one of the decorated newspapers.

"But it's not fair what he says," Nebraska said again. He thought of Benito Marino from New York who had had three excellent shows and whose work was as good as anyone's at the school, including perhaps Bernard's. And Silvers who had even a better eye, yet with not as much taste. But then look at what some of the French students were doing: those who were caught up in the resurgent Lautrec vogue to the extent of actually putting long black gloves on their paintings of the nude models! Even as his fury subsided he knew he could not go back to work at the Académie for a great many days.

Fortunately the next week was warm for early April, bright and without rain. Nebraska finished his water color of the green grocery and the following week had begun another, near Buci, when the weather broke gray and wet and cold as winter. Reluctantly he returned to the Académie which he had not been able to force himself to think about. He arrived during the eleven o'clock break, just as a few of the students were coming across the courtyard. He glanced quickly to see if Anna were among them. He had decided it was not deceit but childishness, perhaps even pride, which had prompted her to show her friends the automobiles. In any case, he would continue as far as possible not to have any serious words with her.

The moment he opened the door, Madame Hélène seized upon him with a false gaiety that made him want to leave. Had she heard about the mock lecture? She, however, was so full of enthusiasm over his appearance (the sun had tanned his bald brow) and over his work outside that he could not discern the direction of her thoughts. She led him away from the ateliers to the foot of the stairs, still talking volubly and louder than usual. Suddenly she stopped, turned and faced him directly and said in a low voice, almost a whisper: "The little Anna, she should not be alone. Ask her to take a cup of coffee with you. That would be very nice of you."

Again he wanted to escape. Were the two women conspiring to force him out of his solitude?

"You know, of course, about her friends, Suzanne and Bernard?"

"No," he said.

"Bernard killed himself. It has been eight days now, Suzanne has gone back to Grenoble to be with her family. Little Anna is alone and naturally quite sad!" Madame Hélène dug into the square pocket of her black smock and asked: "Do you have money for two coffees?" She pulled out a handkerchief and wiped her nose.

He said without moving that he did and that it would be nice if Madame Hélène would join them but she protested that she must finish dinner and find a way of digging out a twenty-franc piece for the little grandson who had stuck it into the window sill. He would find Anna in the still-life room.

Without taking off his raincoat, Nebraska walked through and put away his water colors and brushes on the shelf from which two weeks before he had taken them. The atelier was empty now and without sound. He walked through to the still-life room. In the center, her back toward him, the plump curve of her cheeks showing beyond the small ears, Anna sat gazing at a squash and two eggs. She turned when she heard his steps and smiled pleasantly when she saw who it was. "Look," she said, holding out her sketch pad. "It's lurid no matter what angle you draw from." They regarded the studies and laughed. He was surprised, after Madame Hélène's speech, to find her so cheerful and apparently unchanged. Certainly she would love a cup of coffee—if he had any money, she didn't. They pretended to fight over who should open the door and once across the courtyard who should open the big green doors to the street. Finally, because she had opened the first, she consented to his opening the second.

In the street she said: "You must let me walk on the outside. Next the street." He explained that in America young ladies walk on the inside toward the buildings.

"America, bah!" she said but in a good humor. "Besides it's silly to have such a rule."

"It's because the Elizabethan houses hung over the street and the person walking on the outside was liable to be hit with refuse thrown from above," he explained. "Then too, because the horses splashed mud."

"And here the man gives the woman his left arm, to have her near his heart and to leave his sword hand free to draw and protect her."

"In any case," he said, "you're on the wrong side."

"Do you mind?" she asked gravely. She was walking on the curbstones like a child, balancing, and stepping down occasionally when she could not maintain her balance. "I don't like for people to get between me and the curb."

No, he didn't mind. He was delighted that the conversation was so trivial. During the coffee and the walk back they did not mention Bernard Lévy and the fact that he had killed himself.

In the weeks that followed, the classes went on as before, and if many of the students knew about the suicide no one mentioned it. On sunny days the Académie was almost empty but in rainy weather or on cold days the ateliers were full again. Now in the spring no one could take the work seriously and even the models seemed restless and more bored than usual. Nebraska no longer tried to avoid Anna, who still followed him about like a shy child following a department-store Santa Claus. Whether from fear of her or of himself he did not know, but he did

not want to be alone with her. For that reason he never
stood now, during the breaks, at the door of the Académie
from which he could see the plaque with the engraved
legend of the fallen student. Anna, though, seemed quite
satisfied merely to sit next to him and draw from the same
model and to tease him when his perspective was off.

They were sitting thus, side by side, one cold morning in
late May. The fire was popping in the potbellied stove and
rain was dropping heavily on the skylight. The model before them was a handsome lad with strong nose and cheekbones, a Hamlet haircut, and a square beard that outlined
his prominent jawbone and chin. It was a good face to
draw, easy to catch a likeness of, and excellent for oils. Students had crowded in from the next room where the fat
Negro woman they had drawn all winter was stretched out
in a comfortable but impossible pose. Everyone was working and there was only the sound of the fire, the rain, and
of the charcoal scraping on paper and canvas. Suddenly
the model, who had not twitched a muscle, deliberately
turned his head.

"Ich habe keine Uhr," he said in a deep German voice.
"Um welche Zeit gehen Sie fort?"

For a moment the room was silent. Then regaining his
pose he asked in good Swiss French what time it was, that
he was probably the only Swiss person in the world who
did not have at least one watch.

Several people told him the time and the pencils again
sounded on the tightly stretched canvases. Nebraska himself was measuring the distance from the model's nose to
his bearded chin when he saw out of the corner of his eye
Anna lean forward as though with a stomach cramp. He
watched her hide her face in her hands to try to conceal
that she was shuddering.

"Anna!" he said softly.

She shook her head.

He waited a moment, his fingertips still poised against his canvas. Anna without standing completely up made her way between the stools and easels. When he reached her in the still-life room she was still shaking and the tears in her eyes were held back only by the long lashes.

"What is it?" he asked in English, then in French.

She shook her head from side to side. "Rien. Rien. Nothing." She tried to move away.

He pocketed his pencil. "Let's go get some coffee."

She nodded and walked ahead of him to the vestibule where they put on their coats. Madame Hélène seemed to be not at all aware of their presence or departure, but when Nebraska turned to shut the door he caught her bright eyes regarding him, if not with encouragement or approval, then certainly with understanding.

He did not ask Anna again what the matter was. She walked ahead of him, on the curbstones, and when she had to step down into the street she turned and tried to smile. "I am so silly," she said as though talking about her lack of physical balance. But she continued, first in English which suddenly deserted her and then in French: "If I know the person is a German or I know he is going to speak German, then I'm all right and it doesn't bother me. It's when someone speaks it suddenly, when I do not expect it, that is what makes me tremble all over."

"What are you talking about?" He honestly didn't know.

"The model."

Nebraska realized then that the model had asked a question in German. "But he's Swiss!"

Anna shook her head. "It's silly," she said apologetically. "But I can't help it. I had been sitting there so close to him, studying him so carefully. Not even suspecting that he was sitting there thinking in German!"

In the dark little café they sat quietly for a long while, until finally she was no longer trembling and could look at

him again without embarrassment. "It always makes me
think of the night in 1942 when they were rounding up all
the Jews. My father had already been sent away and my
mother was working in the hospital. In the middle of the
night a neighbor from downstairs who had a key to our door
woke my little sister and me. 'Hurry,' she said, 'they are
here.' My sister and I climbed out onto a roof through a
toilet window and when they went upstairs to get us, the
woman's husband helped us climb down into the alley."

Nebraska drew designs in the spilled coffee on the table
and asked without looking up: "How old were you?"

She had been nine and her sister five. It was July, but it
was a cold night. They had been afraid to be out in the
dark streets and they were afraid to go to any of their
friends' houses because they had been told not ever to say
where they lived or where any of their friends lived if the
Germans ever asked. They had run by back streets down to
the Seine and all night they had walked along the embank-
ments below the street on which the Nazi patrols were
cruising. When the cars passed, they hid under bridges and
for a while they had slept under Pont Alexandre III. At
dawn they were on the Île Saint-Louis and there was a man
in a white trench coat looking down the steps to the river.
They were almost to the top of the steps, intending to ask
his help, when he suddenly spoke, evidently to another
man, in a *urinoir* set into the quai. He had used almost
those same words the model had: *"Um welche Zeit gehen
Sie fort?"*

She and her sister had run past him and down the rue
Saint-Louis. When they looked back the man was coming
toward them, fast. She had not cried and her sister had not
but they knew they were caught. Then suddenly an old,
old woman with two huge baskets, who must have been
watching them, stepped out of a doorway and screamed:

"Ah there you are, you lazy idiots. What do you mean hiding from me? Here, take this basket." And as though they were going over to buy some coal they had, the three of them, walked away from the confused German.

"Thirty thousand Jews were caught that week and packed into the Palais de Sport on Grenelle. That was when Bernard and his family were taken."

"Ah, you knew Bernard before the war?"

"He was the only one who was left. Out of all my schoolmates, he was the only one still alive." She spoke quite matter-of-factly. "You knew he killed himself?"

"Someone mentioned it." Nebraska did not look up. "I was sorry to hear."

She was evidently not convinced or concerned. "Nobody cared. Nobody understood him. Not even me or Suzanne. Suzanne least of all."

"Does anybody know why?"

"He had a cake of soap, you know."

With a real effort Nebraska prevented himself from saying: "But he didn't use it." Instead he raised his eyebrows to question.

"His entire family was taken the same night we got away. They were shipped from the Palais de Sport to concentration camps. His two sisters were sent out in one group, Bernard and the rest of his family in another. He and his mother and father were shipped to the same concentration camp. Bernard was working there in the soap factory and he knew the day his parents were killed so he saved a bar of the soap they were in. We tried to make him throw it away but he wouldn't. He kept it with him all the time. He had it in his hand when Suzanne found him dead."

During the long silence, when the only sound was from distant taxi horns, Nebraska absently traced with the coffee a little two-wheeled toy car on the table. Anna twisted her

head to see it better. "That's for children!" she complained.
"The kind you pedal."

"Yes," he said, still not looking at her. When he did look
up she was laughing. "Do you know why I like to walk on
the curb?" she asked.

Her moods seemed to him to change as fast as those of a
child and certainly her mind darted childlike from subject
to subject.

"Before they carried my father away, my little sister and
I used sometimes to be very frightened. We were so silly.
We didn't know what of, but we would cry. Then he would
take us in his arms and the three of us would sit together in
a big chair and he would tell us that someday we would be
walking down the street and a great big car would stop and
we would get in and we would travel and travel and then
we would be in America and there would be plenty of
everything to eat and plenty of coal to burn to keep warm.
So after that my little sister and I always walked on the
curb one behind the other so we could jump into the car
when it stopped."

Nebraska considered for a long time before he spoke
and when he did his heart stopped beating and choked in
his throat. "Would you like to go to America?"

It was a simple question, but from the solemnity of his
tone and the sudden agitation of his entire body, they both
knew what he was asking and the commitment he was
making.

For a moment she looked frightened and uncertain
whether to speak or not. Finally, deliberately casual, she
asked: "What will you do there?"

"I'll probably teach art in some small Midwestern college."

"But you don't know anything about art." She was

deeply preoccupied and did not seem to know what she was saying. If Nebraska had looked closely he might have recognized that her lips were trying to say yes she would like to go to America but that her sad eyes and querulous brow were asking: "Me? Anna? Grown? Going to America? Married?" She had had to dream, as a child dreams, too long to grow up suddenly into a real world where love and food and warmth were possible. Her face turned furious in the effort to speak but she could say nothing.

"That's true. I know nothing about art." He was breathing now, momentarily relieved that she had not answered his proposal immediately and without contemplation. Until this hour he had not admitted, even to himself, how close he felt toward her, and it would take time to give up entirely all his fears and suspicions of women. He hoped she would give him a few days before saying definitely that she would like to go with him to America. He concentrated studiously on his words: "Perhaps though I can teach them one thing I've learned here and that's a sensible attitude toward art. And maybe I can create, even in just one room, a place where one needn't be embarrassed by talking about painting and by taking it—as, for instance, Bernard did —as a serious part of living. It would have meant a great deal to me when I was growing up to have had such a place."

"Bernard did take it seriously," Anna said. "He used to sit in here by the hour reading newspapers. Whenever he found anything about rebuilding Germany or about what he called fascist tactics in America, he would put it aside and plan for weeks the faces he was going to draw on it."

"I thought he drew on newspapers because he didn't have money enough for paper."

"Money!" Anna said the word evidently louder than she had intended, for she leaned over and her voice was an intense whisper. "Money. You think that's what produces art. You can't separate money from art, and money from morality, and money from politics. That's what's wrong with all of you Americans. But you can separate morality from politics and art from both. Art in one isolated room, indeed!"

The words, which were obviously Bernard Lévy's, sounded ridiculous in Anna's childish voice, but the reference to the isolated room which Nebraska had mentioned in a moment of sentimentality was her own, and the sarcastic tone was her own, and to these Nebraska listened with his old wariness of women. Then had she been playing with him merely to laugh at him? Defeat froze slowly over his eyes which stared without blinking. "Let her laugh," he thought and seemed surprised when she did not.

The silence which separated them now was deep and for five minutes they sat without speaking, each in his own inalterable world.

Finally, quite abruptly, Anna stood up. "It's dark in here," she said, tightening the raincoat belt and making her waist as small and chic and ladylike as possible. But when she walked across the café it was in the heavy tread of a woman already old and weighing two hundred pounds.

"It's strange to realize," she said outside, "that the war is truly over and that I don't really want to go to America." She was holding her head tilted and rather proudly, as women do when they have defeated themselves. She did not need to call his attention to the fact that she was no longer compelled to walk on the curbstone, and, unless that was what accounted for the slight trace of smile on her face, she herself did not seem to be aware that she had chosen to walk on the inside near the buildings, like a young lady.

Whatever it was about them that Madame Hélène observed as they came through the huge green doors and across the mossy courtyard, she did not say directly. For a moment she sat in the oblique sunlight, sad as a toad, and waited for the heavy doors to click shut against the outside noise.

THE RESCUE

He was idling down Piedmont Street, stepping on every line in the sidewalk. If he missed one, didn't step on it, he'd die before he got to the corner.

At the corner he was still alive, and so he paused for a moment, stuck his big toe in the soft tar that filled the crack between the asphalt street and the concrete curb, then ran across.

"I'll count every line on this block." It was just lately he'd started talking to himself, like Crazy Mattie, the vegetable woman who stopped in the middle of the street sometimes to talk to herself, and to dead people, and to God. "I'm not crazy. I just haven't got anybody to talk to . . . four, five, six . . ." One day, about a week after the Fourth of July, he'd counted sixty-three lines, and that was a lot for a boy who just weighed forty-eight pounds. He could have counted more, but old Miss Hallie Thompson

72

who was as deaf as a giraffe had hollered from her porch,
"How's your grandmother? How's your grandmother?
How's your grandmother?" He couldn't tell whether she
heard his answer or not. She just nodded and went back to
reading her newspaper. It looked like an ordinary newspaper to him, but everybody said she read Lips.

He lost count again this afternoon, thinking about Miss
Hallie reading Lips. He took out of his pocket the black
carbon stick from a flashlight battery and drew a long thin
lip on the sidewalk. Then he turned sideways and drew another, smaller, fatter lip in the other direction. It looked
like a T but not very much like one. Then he spelled out,
in regular letters, his name—Ted—the way Miss Clark,
his first-grade teacher, who had a one-legged canary at
home, had taught him.

He stood up and hopped on one leg to the top of the
hill on Piedmont Street. He jumped up on a wall under an
oak tree and sat down to cool between two roots that made
a regular little nest. When he had caught his breath he
jumped up and began clucking like a hen: "Oh, cluck
cluck cluck, look what *I* did. Cluck cluck cluck . . ." He
couldn't cluck like Red Andrews, but he could crow better.
He let out a healthy crow for the city rooster, then cupped
his hands over his mouth and crowed again for the country
rooster who was answering from way off.

Down at the bottom of the hill, across from the lumber
yard where he was headed to play in the sawdust pile, and
next to the filling station where Jake, the Purple-Heart
man, worked, a trailer was parked. It hadn't been there
yesterday, and now all of a sudden here it was. Just like
that. Ted ran down the street and coasted, with a screeching of brakes, to a stop across the street from the trailer.

Three men were out in front, two of them seated on
boxes, watching the third one placing bottles on shelves at
the end of the trailer. A faded sign above the trailer door

said in red letters: "DR. BROWN'S BIGWORD BIGWORD TONIC!"

Warily Ted crossed over, pretending he was going to the filling station. But then when the men didn't notice him, he edged up closer to the group (one of them was Jake) and looked at the bottles. There were flat ones filled with red-brown stuff, and then there were big fruit jars with look-like strips of dough swimming in them.

"What's those things?" His shyness was no match for his curiosity.

"Worms," Jake said. "Out of little boys like you."

Ted looked quickly away so that he wouldn't have a bad dream about them tonight and be fussed at in the morning.

"And this is Worm Medicine," the man with the bottle said. "Dr. Brown's Invigorating Resuscitating Tonic. Finest of its kind."

"Do they like it?" He was fascinated by the idea and planned immediately to watch the worms take the medicine even if it gave him bad dreams.

"Certainly. Sold three bottles to the mayor yesterday."

Ted looked back at the bottles. The big one in the bottle by itself must be the mayor. "What's his name?"

The two seated men laughed. The other, the red-faced ugly man, put the last bottle on the shelf. "Do you think I'm lying to you?" He glared at Ted. "You think I remember the names of all my customers? From the looks of those skinny legs I'd say you need some of this tonic. Tell your mother and father."

"Look behind you, boy!" Jake hollered.

Ted jumped around. There was no lion behind him, only a box covered with screen.

"Nothing but a box," he said.

"Yeah, but look in the box."

He hesitated, then cautiously approached. He looked down into the box. The late-afternoon light coming through the screened top and one screened side was dim, so he dropped down on his knees to see in. There, near a saucer of water, in the one crack of sunlight, a toad sat blinking.

"What d'ya see?"

"A little ole frog."

"What else?" Jake asked.

"Nothing. A saucer and water."

Jake walked over to the box and squinted. He took the boy's head firmly in his big fingertips and turned it toward the opposite corner. "Over there."

"Oh," the boy whispered when he saw the snake. Without moving he was in a deep forest, and there were no men around, no trailer, and no screen between himself and the snake that was looking right at him.

"Two-foot rattler with three rattles," the medicine man said, but his voice did not reach into the deep forest where the child knelt motionless staring at the snake. Sometimes the snake faded into the trees, and the boy would have to squint his eyes to bring it back into view. The sandy swish of car tires passing on the street filtered through the trees and became running water in the forest stream. The snake would brighten until every dark band on his back glowed, then slowly fade again into the darkness. The voices of the men talking were not loud enough to come through the murmuring of the wind in the trees, and the boy would have stayed in the forest forever if the toad had not jumped against the screen.

Ted looked up at the men who were no longer watching him. "Do they like each other?" He didn't see how anybody could like the snake.

"Just like you like ice cream," Jake answered.

"He's going to eat him?" There was an anxious note in the boy's high thin voice.

"Certainly," the medicine man said. "That's what I put him in there for."

The toad jumped again.

"He wants out."

The men went on talking to each other, and no one answered. The boy looked at the box, hoping there was some little hole or little secret door the frog could hop through when the snake wasn't looking. The only way out was through the top, at one corner where the screen had not been tacked down but was merely fastened over the edge with a bent nail.

The toad sat next to the screen now, blinking, his soft underside, chin and stomach heaving in and out like the vacuum cleaner when it's cut on and off real fast.

"Froggy. Froggy." Ted's voice was so high it was almost a whisper. "You're afraid, aren't you, froggy?"

The toad didn't answer, not so you could hear; but the boy could see by its expression, the way its mouth turned down like a pipe smoker's, the way it wouldn't look at the snake, the way it was panting—in all these ways the boy could see that it was scared.

"Let's get him out!" He had to say it three times before the men quit talking. "Let's get the frog out!"

"How?" the medicine man asked.

"He's afraid. Get him out!"

"How?" the man asked in a flat tone.

"*You* get him out!"

"Not me. Not with that snake in there. *You* get him out!"

The two men laughed, and Jake smiled.

"Can I have him if I get him out?"

"Sure. Sure." The medicine man winked at Jake. "Tell you what. I'll get the frog out for you if you'll help me."

"All right," the boy said, excitement rising in his voice. He stood up and walked toward the medicine man.

"All you have to do is hold the snake back while I get the frog."

"Noooo." Ted stopped. He hadn't noticed before that the sun was gone and only the sunset glow remained in the sky.

"Why not?"

" 'Cause. I got to go home." He started toward the street. "I'll be back tomorrow."

He ran up the hill, turning his head every few seconds to watch his dim shadow slanting across the street and racing with him against darkness. Already the sidewalk was losing its heat, and he ran faster. "Lickety-split. Lickety-split all the way home."

He stopped in the side yard, pushed back the tiger lilies (that didn't look like tigers after all of his waiting for them to bloom) and washed his hands at the garden spigot. He dried them on his pants as he slipped across the side porch and into the lighted dining room where his grandmother, aunts, and uncles were already seated at the table.

After supper, after his bath, alone upstairs in bed, he had a thousand ways of going to sleep. Usually he thought about something sad, like the thing he had learned this summer: that everyone in the house, all his aunts and uncles, were more kin to his grandmother than he was; that they were all more kin to each other than they were to him. Or he thought about Jake with a belly full of lead waiting for them to come along with a stretcher, and a red cross, and a Purple Heart. When he thought of things like that he wanted to go to sleep and would not fight the growing heaviness in his eyelids. Tonight he thought about the frog that was kin to nobody in the world.

It was sitting behind the saucer with one eye open watching the snake. It wanted to close both eyes and go to sleep but was afraid to. He held his head behind the pillow and peeped with one eye at the gray square light of window. He let both eyes shut and saw the snake crawling up the

stairs. It made a dry, scraping noise as it crawled. The noise
was the pecan tree brushing against the window screen, but
it was also the snake crawling.

He opened his eyes now and blinked. He drew his knees
up againt his chest and waited. He was breathing slow and
deep like the vacuum cleaner as the snake crawled down
the hall and into the room. He raised his head from behind
the pillow. The pecan tree was no longer scraping; only the
sound of the snake filled the room with its rattling and hissing that was not close or far but all around him. The snake
was crawling around under the bed looking for him. Then
he heard—his body tense for there was no mistake—the
snake wrapping itself around the leg of the bed. Through
the dark, through the pillow and mattress he could see its
head sliding up the post.

If he screamed for help the snake would strike. He slid
down in his bed farther and farther, pulling the sheet up
over him as he moved. He stopped to listen. Once more he
pushed his foot down to move farther away when it struck
the cold, round body of the snake.

"Granny! Granny! Granny!" He screamed it again and
again, not hearing the footsteps on the stairs and in the
hall. When he opened his eyes, the light was on and his
grandmother was pulling the sheet from over him. The iron
bedrail was still there. The snake was gone.

"You play too hard, and you get too tired. That's why
you have all these bad dreams. Today you're to get all your
playing done before noon, and after lunch you're not to go
out of this yard."

They were on the north side of the house. His grandmother was cutting tiger lilies for the dining-room table,
and Ted was between the row of lilies and the house, where
thick moss grew in the dampness from the leaking water
spigot.

With the handle of a tablespoon he was cutting the moss in squares, prying it up and patting it into place on the mud frog-house he had dug and molded on the bank of the drain. As he washed the mud from his hands, he noticed that the water made a river right past the door of the frog-house. The frog would like that.

"Can I have a frog?" He was drying his hands on the seat of his pants.

His grandmother was looking for a lily without too many buds.

"Frogs don't chase chickens. And they don't bark at the garbage man."

"I suppose so. Where're you going to get one?"

"The medicine man," he hollered back as he ran down the drive, his arms churning back and forth like the piston shaft of a train wheel. "The medicine man, medicine-man, medicineman, mediceman, messman, messman, yesmam, yessum, yessm, essm." He blew the whistle, and the train was full steam ahead. "Essm, essm." As he turned up Piedmont Street, the train stopped, to give him time to get his breath and to move the patients to the ambulance. "Arrrunh, arrrrruuunh." On two wheels he turned into Jake's filling station just in time to save the patients, a young couple, from bleeding to death.

"How much?" Jake asked.

"Filler up," Ted answered, pulling up the emergency brakes with a grinding of gears.

"You already owe me two thousand dollars."

"Pay you tomorrow!"

He backed out of the filling station in small, quick steps, circled once and stopped in front of the trailer. The medicine man was sitting on the edge of the unmade bunk, his head between his hands, a whiskey bottle between his feet.

"Good morning," the boy said quietly. The man did not hear so he said in an even softer voice, "I've come after the frog." That done, he went over and lifted the flour sack that was spread over the box.

Sunlight made the cage look larger inside, and the snake smaller. During the night the snake had moved over to the corner behind the saucer of water, away from the opening in the top. The frog was gone.

"He's jumped out." But then Ted saw that the screen was still fastened with the sharp end of the nail that had been driven from the inside of the box. He dropped to his knees and shaded his eyes from the sun glare. In the little triangle between the snake and the corner of the box, the frog was sitting, still blinking, still breathing, in and out, in and out. "Uh, oh!" Ted spoke with his mouth still open in amazement.

He looked about for a stick long enough to reach in and make the frog jump away from the snake, but thin enough to go between the wires of the screen. Wild onion shoots were not long enough; peach switches were too big around. He scooped up a handful of sand and let it funnel through his tight-clasped fist onto the frog. The frog moved a few inches away but did not hop; then it sat motionless. Ted picked up another handful and threw it with stinging force through the screen. Both the snake and the frog moved.

The frog hopped twice and landed in the middle of the cage. The snake moved only its head, sliding it along the sandy floor until it touched the saucer. It lifted its tail and shook the rattles in a short, angry warning. It lifted its head from behind the saucer and darted its tongue in and out.

Ted poured another handful of sand in a steady stream onto the frog. It jumped once more so that it was now almost under the opening in the top of the cage. The snake's flat head weaved back and forth, and the rattles now hummed steadily, like a katydid on the first cool nights of autumn when school has started and the circus is coming to town.

The boy was on his knees now before the box. The distances, he figured, were in his favor. He twisted the bent nail and slipped the screen wire loose. He bent the wire back and held his hand poised in the opening, watching the snake, the frog, his hand, the snake—and breathing not at all. Quickly he thrust his hand into the box. He grabbed the frog. He had it and was pulling out his hand when the snake struck, and missed.

He didn't hear himself scream, nor feel the bent nail point as it tore his skin from elbow to wrist. He only felt the wet frog struggling to be free and saw the snake, crawling and coiling, in sudden curves.

"My God, boy! Get away from there!" The medicine man was holding on to the door of the trailer and was the color of the pale worms that floated in the bottles on each side. "Get away! You wanta be killed?"

Ted stood up. His knees were trembling; he'd been stooping so long. He turned and started toward the street, holding the frog in the palms of his cupped hands. If Jake hadn't called at that moment, he would have been sick.

Jake was running toward him. "Did it bite you? Let's see your arm there. Hold up, Ted."

He turned and started back toward Jake. The sun was so hot and white that he was dazed. Jake led him into the filling station. "Did the snake do that? Did the snake do that?"

"No. I did it on that old nail."

"No. I don't suppose a snake could do all that." Jake laughed his forced laugh, now that he knew. "Better put something on it anyway." He was getting out a flat tin box with a red cross on it. Outside the medicine man was trying to fasten the screen on the box without bending over. He was mumbling to himself.

"Now where're we going to put the frog while we fix your arm? Let's see now," Jake said, looking on the shelf, where he kept the Purple Heart, for an empty cigar box.

"I don't want him any more." Ted spoke gravely.

"Don't want him any more?" Jake was still laughing each time he spoke and searching the boy's face for tears. "Why, you'll want him soon as we get that old arm of yours all doctored up."

"No. Let's turn him free."

"All right," Jake said. He studied the boy's face. "If that's what you want. It's yours."

They walked out to the side of the filling station away from the snake cage. There, in the shadow of a stone back of the air pump. Ted set the frog on the ground. As Jake spread the iodine up and down the long scratch on his arm, the boy watched the frog jump across the wire grass and into the wild strawberries growing in the shade of the oak. Each time it jumped, the boy wanted to laugh and cry at the same time, but he could not because he was not alone.

He turned and watched Jake's large hand dip the glass rod back into the bottle, and watched the wrinkles deepen on Jake's face.

"Jake," he asked, "how much kin am I to you?"

THE GLASS-BRICK
APARTMENT

They tell me here that it sometimes helps to remember events accurately and to see them all again. I was ten the summer my Uncle Nat was taken away sick and I was not to talk about it with any of the neighbors.

Four years before that summer when I came to live with my grandparents, Uncle Nat had moved out of his upstairs room to the basement where he'd made a cool, dry apartment for himself. It was the time in the early thirties when everything was Modern—meaning, in the South, glass-brick. Uncle Nat, by saving each week, had managed during two years to replace the old sunbaked bricks with glass ones. The lot sloped from the street to the creek and the apartment had full-sized windows, the sills of which were a good two feet above the garden path. Often he stood, very tall and bony, looking out the big plate glass window at the garden and the stream.

My grandmother was against the idea of the apartment from the very beginning. Uncle Frank, her oldest son, had been killed in France; Uncle Charles had left home when he was sixteen, and no one knew where he was; Fred, the youngest, my father, came only at Christmas time. Uncle Nat was the only one left. Except for two years at the university, he had lived all his life in a room across from my grandmother's. The room had a high ceiling and a ceiling fan, and one of Uncle Nat's toy airplanes still hung from the center of the fan and circled slowly when the fan was turning. He and my grandmother had fought every day for two months while he and Will Jason, a Negro who had worked for him at his florist before it was closed by the Depression, were wallboarding the basement.

"Living in a basement!" my grandmother seemed to say at least once every day. "If you don't come down with consumption, it'll be something worse."

I remember one day when she said it, we were in the front parlor and she was standing in the tall windows which reached from floor to ceiling, fussing with the dark, red velvet drapes. Uncle Nat was standing by the door with a cup of flour he had come up to borrow.

"What's worse?" I asked, hoping for descriptions of a tropical disease so horrible I could not go to sleep.

"Living at home," Grandpa said. He loved Grandmother and Uncle Nat, but not when they were together.

"Why," I whispered to Grandpa, "is living at home worse?"

He fingered his empty pipe and glanced up through his white brows. When he winked I knew he meant: "Later, when we walk down to Five Points for the evening paper."

She had seen him wink. "Make him think of his mother." She jerked the drapes and the brass rings jumped along the grass rod. "Make him homesick."

But Grandpa and I had talked about it the first time my

grandmother slapped me. He knew I was glad that my
mother was keeping books for some peach growers and
that I was here for the summer. I was glad that my parents
were getting separation papers and that in the fall my
mother and I would have a very small apartment in a large
apartment house with balconies and with a policeman at
the corner. My father couldn't bother us then.

"Have you written your father?" Grandmother asked.
She had opened my last letter from him and knew that he
didn't like living alone. She believed it when, at the end of
the letter, he promised to quit drinking. She didn't know
him like I did. My father had gone off to school and had
married without returning. "He didn't get away soon
enough," my mother used to say. "Still he's better off than
Nat." She never said why. To keep now from telling Grandmother that I had written him, I asked: "Why is Daddy better off than Uncle Nat?"

"Who told you that?" She seemed taller when she walked
under the glass beads of the chandelier to the dark mantel.
I looked to Grandpa for help, but he was studying his pipe.

"You see what she's been telling him?" Grandmother
said. Here, "she" meant my mother; at home, "she" meant
my grandmother.

"Why do you call her 'She'?" I asked. "Don't you know
her name?"

She could hear the anger in my voice. "Careful how you
talk to me," she said. "You're getting a little too smart to
suit me."

I hated her. At that moment when she turned and started
out of the room, stiff and proud, I thought again how I
wanted to take my BB gun and shoot at her in her stiff
corsets.

Grandpa and Uncle Nat were watching me and I was
afraid they could see what I was thinking. Uncle Nat
smiled, not much, but enough to show the edges of his

large, even teeth. "How do you like living in my old room?"

I told him I liked the fan and the airplane and the army-boy adventure books left over from when he was a little boy.

"He's still a little boy," Grandpa said.

Uncle Nat quit smiling. He stared at my grandfather a while before he finally said: "Like father, like son." Sometimes it was no better here than it was at home. Just when you were all set to like everybody, they didn't like each other. Uncle Nat walked out of the room and the door to his stairs clicked shut.

Grandpa shook his head. "Forty years old and still single and still living at home." While Grandpa played with his empty pipe, I sat on the arm of his chair. When I saw that he was not going to say anything else, I asked him my question again: "Which'd you rather be run over by: an old Greyhound bus or a new one?" He still hadn't answered that one.

I remember that later that summer Uncle Nat and I were at the foot of the garden when he asked me in a funny voice: "How did your mother treat your father?"

He was sitting on an old broken-down wicker chair and wore only a pair of khaki shorts and dirty white sneakers. His skin was as brown as the hair on his chest and legs. He'd been clipping hedges but had stopped to sweat. All he did now that the florist was closed was to tend the garden, sometimes with Will Jason, but usually by himself.

I was washing marbles in a sand pool in the creek. We'd been talking about where I lived and how many rooms and things like that when he asked me that question in a funny voice.

"Sir?" I said. I didn't know how to answer. My father was my father, and mother my mother, and nobody "treated" anybody anyway. "I don't know."

"It's none of my business," he said. "I shouldn't have asked."

"Grandpa says you ought to get married."

"Maybe that's why I was asking."

"You're going to marry Mother?" I glanced at him. It would be funny to have to call him "Daddy." I grinned. He looked a little like my father.

"Why're you laughing?" He frowned.

"I'd have to call you 'Uncle Daddy' then."

"I'm old enough to have a son your age." He quit frowning. "I'm old enough to have a son ready to go off to the university."

"Would he live in the basement with you?" I still hadn't been in his apartment. When I was sure he wasn't there, I would peep through the plate glass window and try to see why he kept it all locked and secret.

"What?" he asked, already way off.

He was staring across the garden and creek at the woods. I watched and listened too. The late morning sun was slanting through the water oaks and willows and lighting up the crape myrtle and the water where it foamed white around the wet green rocks. A white butterfly was flicking under the bushes and over the water and up over the rocks. A swarm of gnats hung near the moss bank and moved, the whole cloud of them, in sudden jerks, up, then settled slowly back.

"It's all got by so fast," he said. "A man thinks life is going to be . . ."

I waited. His lips moved but I could hear only bee noises from the crape myrtle, and from the woods beyond, noon noises, hot and still.

He looked so much like my father I felt, for the first time, kin to him; and I felt the same kind of shyness I felt when my father was happy-drunk. But when I tried to sit on the arm of his chair he jumped up. The chair fell over and landed on top of me. He did not try to lift it off, but stood over me, whispering through the wicker, as if I were a wild animal in a cage: "Don't touch me!"

I lay in the grass under the wicker chair, unhurt, but wanting to cry and not to cry. I was not stunned, but I was not breathing.

"Crazy! Crazy! All of you are crazy!" I wanted to shout as he hurried toward his apartment under the house. That's what my mother said to my father and to me, too, when I lost my temper. Instead, I said, not loud enough for him to hear: "I don't want to touch you."

I was embarrassed for him and for myself. Breathing again, no longer needing to cry or not to, I wanted only to get out from under the chair and across the stream and to sit in the dugout which my father and uncles had dug when they were young.

My grandmother had seen it all, just as she saw everything. Already she was rapping on his window, and, not seeing him, was coming down the garden path toward where I lay under the chair. As she stepped through the flower border and onto the grass, she called to me: "What did you do to him?"

"What?" I asked, standing up with the chair between her and me.

"Don't you say 'what' to me!"

"Ma'am?" I asked.

"What did you put on him?" She studied the chair as though she expected to see a snake or a lizard or a tadpole. I could not tell her that I had merely wanted to put my hand on his shoulder, that sitting there he looked sad and like my father. I could tell her nothing.

"You're more trouble," she said, "than all my four sons put together."

I wanted to say, "You go to hell." But I just stood there, out of her reach, and let her stare at me and I stared right back into her gray eyes without blinking. I pressed my lips together tight to let her know how much I hated her and how much I wished she were dead. We stared without moving.

Behind me I could see the water white against the stones and could see again the white butterfly skimming the water, but all the time I was staring into her gray eyes knowing I would not be the first to look away.

The bee noises sounded at one moment far off and the next moment inside my head and the garden was so bright my eyes seemed shut and this was a picture of a garden burned on my eyelids. My grandmother was a black shadow standing like a paper doll against the bright garden and I was a paper doll too, swaying backward and forward. I kept my lips pressed tight and made spit back of my teeth with the tip of my tongue. If she moved toward me, I'd spit on her. But she did not move and I could not.

After a while she was no longer black nor the garden so bright nor the bees so close in my head. But we didn't move. What if we were to die here like this? What if we never moved? The grass would grow tall around our legs. Then it would snow and the snow would pile up and maybe bury us.

Her face was twitching now. A muscle in her cheek was jumping. I wanted to laugh. But I thought about how much I hated her. "You won't break my spirit." I had heard the words somewhere and about my grandmother. "You won't break my spirit, you won't break my spirit you won't . . ." I said over and over till the words ran together in the glare and hot silence like pats of butter and I could both see and hear them but they had no meaning because she was staring and her eyes ran together like the pats of butter and the words and there were her eyes in the pool of butter and my marbles in the sand pool and the words and bee noises in my head. The garden was bright, then dark.

After a long time the garden turned bright again and there was a sob in my throat. I could not swallow now. My right knee was trembling and I felt like I was going to sit down without wanting to. She did not move.

I couldn't cry now or sit down or run away. I didn't know what to do. I dried my palms against my wet shorts and remembered to press my lips together again, tight, to show her how much I hated her though now I didn't hate her as much. Now I could imagine leading her down to show her the marbles in the sand pool and pressing up close to her and smelling the dusty lemon odor of her starched dress. I said it over and over: "I hate you I hate you . . ." But the words lost their meaning and left me with nothing to keep my face mean and my lips tight and my backbone stiff. "It's a silly game we're playing," I said to myself, "and I can quit any time I want to." I could feel a smile in my eyes and I wondered would she know it was a silly game and that we could quit. I could feel the smile on my lips.

She lifted her chin and the line from the corner of her nose to the corner of her mouth deepened. It was not a smile and not a sneer, but a proud look as though she'd won. "It's a good thing you changed your mind," she said. She lifted her head higher and picked her way through the border and up the walk.

I hadn't lost. I hadn't looked away. I was still standing there in the same spot. She hadn't won, she hadn't! I wanted to pick up a rock and throw it at her. I wanted to run across the stream and sit in the dugout. My knees were trembling and I sat down in the grass and tried to think about nothing, not even about the ant that was crawling up a blade of grass and waving its feelers against the air. I bent my head low and asked it my question: "Which'd you rather be run over by: a new Greyhound bus or an old one?"

In late August the dime store windows were full of notebooks and yellow pencils. In three weeks school would be starting and I was homesick. Uncle Nat was acting funny and hardly spoke to me at all. He wouldn't come into the garden if I was playing in the creek and he wouldn't come upstairs if I was in the house. He had, though, one day when I was in the dugout, come up to his room and taken the toy airplane. I didn't care but I wouldn't even look through his window to see if he had it hanging up in his apartment.

My grandfather would walk me down to Five Points and explain that it was not my fault but to stay out of Grandmother's way because she was worried and sleepless about Nat. The only thing I heard her say about it though was: "I wish we could afford Will Jason one day a week. He could get Nat interested in gardening or in something, I believe." But Grandpa said he didn't think Mr. Robins would let Will come and add the cost to the unpaid drug bill. "I don't know how much longer he'll let me have pipe tobacco."

Twice I wrote to my mother to come and get me, but I didn't tell her that my grandmother and Uncle Nat would hardly speak to me. She had written back that the last peaches had been shipped and that next week she would go into town and have the furniture moved and would send for me.

I wrote and told her please to send now. I wouldn't be in the way. Please, I could help her with the furniture if she would send for me. I didn't mention what was happening to Uncle Nat and how my grandparents were worried. The next evening she telephoned long-distance and explained that it would be easier her way, that I'd been a brave boy all summer and couldn't I be brave a week or so longer? She spoke to Grandpa and then to me again.

"Yes," I had to say, even with my grandparents listening. "Yes. I know you love me."

Then, because she kept asking, I had to say with them listening: "I love you too." But then I couldn't say "good-bye" when she said "goodbye." She waited for me to say something or to hang up and finally she said, "Hang up, darling." I could hear my breath in the phone and could smell the dusty telephone smell, but I couldn't say anything.

"Hang up, darling," she said. "So I can hang up too." I knew she meant it was costing money but I couldn't say "Goodbye." I put the receiver back on the hook and went upstairs without speaking to my grandparents who were watching me and lay down on the rug in the middle of the room and studied the string dangling from the fan.

The rest of the week I stayed away from the house as much as possible. In the mornings I worked on the dugout; but when I started back to the house for a plank, I could see Uncle Nat standing in the garden, not with a hoe or mallet, but just standing. Then when I would come out on the creek bank he would be gone.

The next week there was a cool breeze across the garden every morning. The sky was September blue and clear all day without a cloud. One noon when I was hopping across the stream, late for lunch, I heard shouting near the house. I stepped back and waited, not hiding, but not in plain view. Uncle Nat was walking back and forth shouting up at the house: "I'll be damned if they do!"

He ran into his apartment and slammed the door. No one was in the yard, but then I saw my grandmother's head in the kitchen window. I turned and started back to the dug-out, but thinking that she had perhaps seen me, turned again, and jumped from stone to stone across the creek.

Lunch was not ready. The green beans had burned to the bottom of the pot. The kitchen was full of smoke. In the dining room the ice tea was poured and the ice already melted. In the kitchen my grandparents were both talking at once in sudden spurts, then they were quiet, then talking again, one, then the other, then both, too excited to finish anything.

Sitting in the dining room behind the swinging door, I finally understood: my father had lost his job a month ago. My mother had discovered it when she went for the furniture. He could not afford an apartment for her or for himself. My grandparents had no money to send her. The money from her summer job would feed us for a while, but would not be enough for rent. She was giving my father fifty dollars so that he could go to California where he claimed he could get a job. She would have to come here to live.

Grandpa began in a loud voice: "Then she'll have to take an upstairs room . . ."

"I will not have her telling me . . ."

"All right, then." Grandpa's voice dropped and was calm. "What else can we do?"

"Nathan's got to listen to reason." Grandmother's voice was full of anger and tears.

"And what *is* reason?" he asked in an even, calm voice as though he were talking to a baby.

"He'll have to move back upstairs and let them have the basement."

"That's what you wanted all along." His voice was angry again. "Isn't it?" I could hear him push back a chair and walk to the window.

"Don't say that's what I want!" Grandmother said. Suddenly her voice dropped and she said quietly, "I'm trying to do what's best for everybody."

"Poor Nat," Grandpa said. "It's all he has . . ."

"Besides"—my grandmother's anger was back—"two women cannot live in the same house together. This way she'll have hers, I'll have mine."

Again there was shouting in the yard. Uncle Nat was

under the kitchen window. "I knew it! I knew when I was painting this goddamn basement that Fred would get it."

"Fred's going to California for God's sake!" Grandpa hollered out the window.

"That's right," my grandmother said. "Tell the neighbors."

"They're not going to have it. I'll burn it first." The basement door slammed shut.

"If she'll sell most of that awful, new-looking furniture," my grandmother was saying, but I didn't listen to the rest. I drank a glass of warm tea and took two corn muffins which had already been split and buttered and went out the front door and through the side yard to the creek and across it to the dugout.

Late that afternoon when I came back up through the garden, I could see Uncle Nat standing in the exact middle of the big window. The curtains were drawn on either side of him and he stood without moving. I tried not to look at him, but I kept glancing up. If I told him it wasn't my fault, that I didn't want his old basement . . . if I told him we'd move out as soon as my father got a job . . . but that wouldn't fool him . . . it didn't even fool me. Shoot! He couldn't even hold a job here.

But I was trying to think of words to say in case he stepped out and blocked the path. He was staring, though, at something way above my head, off in the woods. I wanted to turn to see what he was seeing, but I kept on walking up the path and around the house without stopping.

As I went to sleep that night a wind was scraping oak leaves against the window screen and across the slate roof. Once in the night I was half awake and heard voices in the hall. Grandmother and Uncle Nat were talking and she was saying: "I'm glad you changed your mind."

During breakfast the next morning my grandparents did not speak. In the silence I planned what I would say to Uncle Nat if I had a chance. I wouldn't mention his apartment, my father, or anything about where we were going to live. I'd simply tell him about the new steps to the dugout. If he wanted to go and look at them, he could go with me.

As soon as my grandmother folded her napkin, I asked to be excused and ran down, hoping to find him in the garden. He was still standing between the curtains, staring over my head at the same spot in the woods. He did not move. Had he been standing there all night? Had I dreamed the wind and the voices in the hall?

"Uncle Nat," I said, not loud. He did not hear. "Uncle Nat," I said with more breath, then softer. "You want to see the dugout?"

Still he did not move. I stood close to the window. His eyes were open but he was not blinking them. I tapped on the window to make him blink, to make him look at me. "Uncle Nat!" I called.

He did not blink. He was still staring. I rapped louder. "Uncle Nat!" I could not see him breathing either. "He's dead!" I thought. I moved back from the window and screamed: "Grandpa!"

Both my grandparents came to the kitchen window, but I could not look up or away from Uncle Nat standing between the curtains staring out at that spot in the woods, not blinking, not breathing.

"What is it?" they were both asking but I couldn't tell them or look away. With my grandparents coming down the steps I was no longer afraid. I knew he was not dead. "Uncle Nat," I tapped on the glass. "Uncle Nat."

Then, behind me, my grandfather said: "Oh, my God."

My grandmother pushed me aside. "Nat," she called. She cupped her hands on each side of her face and peered into the window, a foot away from his face. "Nathan," she said firmly. She stepped back, but he was still staring at the spot in the woods.

"Well," Grandpa said. He was looking at my grandmother as though they both knew something. "This is it."

My grandmother's face had no expression, nor did her voice when she turned back and rapped on the window. "Nat, answer me."

"We'll have to get in," Grandpa said. They were almost whispering but they did not sound afraid, or sad, or anything. They could have been talking about potatoes. "Have you got a key?"

"You'll have to use the skeleton key. It's under the scarf on my dresser." As my grandmother spoke she did not look away from the window, but she said louder, as though she could see Grandpa rounding the path by the corner of the house: "You'll have to go in from the upstairs door." She turned to me. "Run down to Five Points. Tell Mr. Robins to send Will Jason."

"What if . . ." I began.

"Tell him I said to," Grandmother said, firmly, but quietly.

"What if he wants to know why?"

"Tell him Nathan's sick," she said. "Don't tell anybody else."

As I passed Grandpa he said: "Run, boy. Run." And I said the words to myself all the way to the drug store.

The next evening everything was settled. A doctor was in the hall making one last phone call. My grandparents were on the side porch trying to close the bent top of a Thermos full of hot coffee. Will Jason was carrying a basket of food to the black U-Drive-It car parked in the driveway. Grandpa and Will Jason would drive all night and be at the state hospital by eight o'clock the next morning. Uncle Nat sat in the front seat staring straight ahead at the street. I stood back of the car, watching.

I wanted to tell Uncle Nat that we didn't want his apartment. I wanted to tell him something to make him laugh. If he would smile, even a little, he could, I knew, quit staring and begin moving again. If they let me stare back at him, I could get him to smile. Or if I could think of something to tell him. But he knew all my jokes and riddles. He knew about the Greyhound bus. I even thought of poems and rhymes I knew and movies I had seen and about the new steps to the dugout.

I moved around the side of the car away from the house and stood near the front window where he sat staring. I didn't try to stand on the running board because he might think I wanted to touch him again. I moved on up to the front of the car, still trying to think of something to say. He didn't seem to notice me. I eased up on the bumper and onto the front fender and lay down across the hood so that he would have to turn his head if he didn't want to be staring at me through the windshield. The street light was reflecting from the windshield but on the other side I could see his eyes still looking straight ahead. Then I said the rhyme I knew:

> Say, little boy!
> Where'd you get your britches?
> Your mama cut the pattern out,
> Your papa sewed the stitches!

Uncle Nat didn't move. But Will Jason came up to my side and said: "What're you doing up there?"

"I'm telling him a rhyme I know."

Will Jason began lifting me off the hood. "I don't think he'll appreciate it," he said. He set me on the ground. Then he watched my grandfather on the porch shaking hands with the doctor. Will Jason walked around to the driver's side and opened the door. He leaned into the car and said: "We'll be on our way in a minute, Mr. Nat."

A CARACOLE IN PARIS

Later, after the blood had been properly shed, I realized what I had always known: all it takes for melodrama is two Southerners.

The Embassy estimated there were ten thousand Americans living that year on the Left Bank. But Mary David Clark was the only Southern woman I met in Paris; and so far as anyone seemed to know, I was the only man there from the Deep South.

I had had, a few weeks before meeting Mary David, a final, spectacular fight with a rather beat and bustless French girl named Denise who lived at Montparnasse. To avoid seeing her, I had found a café on the Place St. Sulpice, near the cathedral itself.

It is there one morning that I first hear Mary David Clark. She is speaking English in the most wonderful of delta accents. Her words, slow as the river, delight me; I

99

smile inwardly, without taking my eyes from the article I am translating for a New York law firm. I do not want, in my present mood, to meet her, or any woman from anywhere; but there is no harm, I think, in letting the soft, familiar words pour over and about me.

"Heah we wuh," she is saying, "sittin' on the dining cah." She describes in charming detail the car, the passengers, the rock walls passing by, the stone houses and runted apple trees. I glance up to see a thin woman, probably about five years older than myself, say about forty, neat in a crisp brown linen suit.

The man she is talking to is eagle-like in his sharpness, and could be anywhere between thirty and forty-five. He catches my eye, knows I am listening, just as I know he is not. His face is one I have seen vividly somewhere.

". . . and all these American tourists on the dining cah wanting to know if this is Normandy or Brittany and every last one ashamed to ask. So the next time that cute little waiter comes prissing up I said in my best Alabama French, 'Is this Normandy or Brittany, sir?' In French, of course, and he said, "It's cauliflower, Madame, choufleur,' and put another spoonful on my plate."

The eagle-faced man laughs without true amusement; his intense pale-blue eyes are ceaselessly scanning the square and terrace for moving prey. I have seen him before in some unpleasant circumstance.

She is almost whispering: "That was four days ago and I haven't spoken one word of French since then."

"How do you manage?" His eyes follow coldly the muscular thighs of Robert, the young waiter, who in his shiny tight pants is pirouetting in and out among the chairs.

"English," she says. "If you speak English plainly enough and slowly enough, anybody in the world can understand you."

The next morning I am there in time to see her come out

of the hotel on the square and cross to the fountain where she shakes crumbs out of a napkin for the pigeons strutting and bobbing at her feet. She wets her fingertips in the fountain pool and turns round and round, leisurely drying her fingertips on the napkin and studying the plane trees and the unclouded sky.

With one hand she is clasping now a camel's-hair coat in cape fashion about her shoulders; and with the other she swings with a reserved abandon a beautifully worn leather satchel. She turns slower and slower, evidently astonished still and pleased to find herself here, at last, alone, at the beginning of adventure, in the heart of Paris.

In the authoritative way she surveys the mansard rooftops, in the proprietary way she scatters the pigeons of St. Sulpice, one can see the headstrong person she has always been: the tomboy riding a mare with mane as roan as her own straight hair across a gravel drive to shout for ice water from an overworked Negro cook or a bullied stepmother. Refused, she caracoles in the jonquils until a glass is fetched and a pitcher. And years later, caracoling through a short marriage with a lieutenant who comes back from a Middle East tour, but not to her. Her divorce almost undoes her thousand relatives in Montgomery and Troy and perturbs even her father in his bedside manner where charm heals perhaps more than his licensed ignorance can kill.

She comes across the square, her ghosts in file: the not-quite sorority girl, not-quite debutante, not-quite garden-club lady, the not-quite wife, the not-quite virgin old maid. And by paradox, she who is not-quite anybody gives as the result of that same breeding the appearance of being completely at home everywhere. Graciously she steps aside and allows the domestics in their saddest black coats to trudge the mica-flecked pavement of her square and even to disturb with their heavy shopping bags the gathering storm of her pigeons.

Thus she arrives and settles herself and tells Robert in her "perfectly good English" that she wants coffee, bread, and butter. As he attends her he becomes a real though virile dandy, adjusting chairs with sharp clicks and wiping tables with smart flicks of his towel. Inside, waiting for the coffee, he tightens his bow tie, tugs his short white jacket. Few have seen Robert smile before but he smiles this morning as he places the coffee before Mary David. Even Robert can not resist the smile of a freckle-faced woman.

Much later, when I rest my eyes again, I see she has taken from her satchel a pad, a sort of bamboo fountain pen with a secret source of ink, and is sketching the lions of the fountain, the pillars of the church, the dome with its copper-green pelican plucking its metal breast for blood, the iron grillwork at the base of the trees, the Vespesian, even the heavy Cinzano ashtrays, all with great speed and a minimum of detail. Robert draws closer to admire the results of her noisy scratchings. He is obviously proud that the new customer is, in addition to being a gentlewoman, an artist as well.

When the sun begins to hit my paper and writing hand, I look up from my translating and am surprised to see the eagle-faced man standing at Mary David's table. He is trying to see the sketches on her pad, but she has flung her hand out casually across them. She says: "No. You mustn't look, I'm sorry. They're croissant. Café au lait. Gendarme. Concierge. All that."

"What do you mean, they are all croissant?" Today I can hear: his accent is Germanic. And like all Germans when they are being obtuse, he lets his voice become thick and guttural, making up in force what it lacks in intelligence. "You have drawn croissants and gendarmes?"

"I've drawn a picture of que voulez-vous." She motions that he should sit down rather than take what he obviously hopes is an informal stance but that suggests rather a soldier at attention, who intends to scratch his armpit the second the sergeant's back is turned.

She explains: "They're sketches of the square . . . the cathedral."

"And your concierge?" He sits quickly and clicks on her cup with a spoon to summon Robert.

"Not literally. Before I came here I got so tired of reading and hearing about Paris from people who had to throw in every word of guidebook French they knew: apéritifs, rues, and pensions. You know, and if they're really with it, they throw in a merde every page or so. That's what these drawings are: guidebook sketches. Something every tourist who's been here a week knows."

"But it is for your Americans. This is fabric you design, isn't it?"

She says: "Certainly. But Americans are more sophisticated now. They don't want the Eiffel Tower on their shower curtains. It's a competitive business." It is strange to imagine this slow-talking woman in the competitive world of fashion and design. "Nobody's going to catch me on a hardtop road."

He settles back and suddenly swells his chest as if he is about to light a cigar. "The apartment I promised you. It is yours."

Apparently she does not understand how hard apartments are to find, what an impossible thing this man has done for her. "I have only to go to his lawyers on the rue de Rennes to sign the lease and the inventory."

"I searched as I crossed the square. I couldn't tell which it is but there's an adorable one up above here," she points with the bamboo pen over her shoulder, "very chic with a boxwood hedge."

"That is the precise one!" He wants me, everyone, to see his joy, what a bright man he is. His pale eyes take in the street, the terrace, and stop again at me. His smile dissipates. I return his stare which becomes a hostile glint.

Now I know where I have seen him before: at the gate of the American Embassy, circulating a petition to stop our meddling in Asian affairs. He has put on some weight since then, but the harsh angularity is there, the skull head, the nose that could be Roman, Jewish, or hawk. It is said he was in a concentration camp; but Denise who was with me at the Embassy said simply: "If he was in a concentration camp I am certain he was a guard. He's a Nazi. And on his way to being a psychotic. If he'd find himself a boy friend he'd know what his trouble is. Maybe then he could relax before he goes completely mad." She speaks with the authority of one who has not wasted her childhood reading anything lighter than Krafft-Ebing, though in fact all her judgments, like the best from Frenchwomen, are from instinct.

Mary David, however, seems to be finding nothing strange in his manner, and seems even a little charmed by him. But she is Southern, woman, alone in a foreign city; and he has found her an apartment. Still, I can imagine easily her confiding in me, after she has the key to the apartment and a knowledge of the community: "Honey, he's got this peculiar odor. I don't know whether it's that awful skin rash or those clothes he sponges himself, but he smells so much like kerosene I'm afraid to strike a match near him." I will agree that she can't have somebody like that around who might blow up at any moment, and she'll pull on her velvet ax-gloves and say: "I mean he's sweet and he saved me a lot of rent by leasing the apartment in his name and all that and he's certainly been a perfect gentleman. . . ." And she'll be the perfect lady and he'll never even see the ax blade coming down.

He is being a perfect gentleman now. He leans forward and shows her the price written on a card. Then, as if he has offended me by his exclusive whisper, he leans back and smiles seductively at me. It is that dangerous latent smile which Denise observed and which a man, even without a warning, does not return without risking an outright accusation of flirting. He continues the smile until it becomes a stare, a dare, and then a mockery. Yes, it is the same man who made a scene at the Embassy by shouting that all American men are perverted. There should be some way to warn this compatriot, this unbeguiling Southern woman, that she is dealing with a potentially mad man.

He looks deliberately away and leans forward and whispers something to Mary David. She waits an appropriate moment before glancing my way. Now I am the one who feels perverted, politically suspect, paranoid. He gulps his coffee and with a Germanic briskness, a clicking of cup to saucer, chair to table, heels to terrace, shakes her hand and leaves.

Before he is out of sight she says to me: "Do you know that man?" Her voice is easy, lazy with me, as if she knows I will speak with a Southern accent too.

"I've seen him around," I say.

"He doesn't live near here," she half explains, half questions.

"I've seen him near the Embassy."

"Do you know anything about him?" she says. "I just met him through a friend on the boat and I don't know anything at all about him. Except his name: Kretzer."

I laugh suddenly. This might as well be Opelika, Alabama, after church. "You mean you don't even know what his daddy does?"

She laughs. "Honey, I don't even know who his granddaddy was and where his folks come from, much less who they're *related* to."

We look at each other fondly. We speak the same language. Later we can give all the unnecessary and similar pages of our biographies. We are both, I am sure, optimistic about the outcome of the struggle in the South, sure of a new prosperity there for everyone, annoyed with the Northern press, bored to hell and back with aggressive Yankee liberals who will continue to discover in superb innocence what we have protested for fifteen or twenty years.

"What about him?" she asks.

"I think he's borderline psychotic." It is strange to be quoting Denise still and still with perfect confidence in her intuitions.

She feints. She wants not to hear. "I think he's sweet. He's gone to lease an apartment for me. He couldn't be sweeter."

"I think he may be dangerous," I say. Maybe later she will tell him what I've said; but at least I will have done my duty, whatever happens.

"You really think so," she asks.

"I really think he's on the verge of violence."

"Violent," she says slowly. The word lights up the sky and in its peculiar light everything in sight becomes magic to her. I have said the wrong thing. She is committed to him now. "You really think he might be violent." Again sheet lightning whitens the square and engraves the cathedral against the sky.

"I think," I try again, "he is insane."

"Oh, I don't think that," she says. "I think he's just a little nuhvous."

She pulls the camel's-hair coat about her shoulders; and I cannot tell whether it is the word nervous or the word violent that brings a slight and rather attractive shiver to her wide shoulders.

The rest of the day I am a little uneasy and I cannot tell whether I am about to become infatuated with Mary David or be caught up in another bout of homesickness. At any rate, I hope she heeds my words. But that afternoon, unable to stay away, I return to the square and see them moving her luggage from the hotel, across the square, and through the grilled gateway in the building next to the Vavin Café.

As I stand on the cathedral steps in the late afternoon sun, I wonder if this uneasy feeling I have is fear, or jealousy, or lonesomeness. One thing I'm sure of: I will not go back to the Vavins' café. Maybe I will go back to Montparnasse. By now Denise will have found a Frenchman "who understands tenderness" and perhaps gone with him to another quarter.

It is a long time before I see Mary David again. Winter has come and is worse than the winter before. Mary David, huddled deep in a leather and fur coat, is walking with Kretzer through the bright bare alleys of the Luxembourg. From the upturned collar of his greatcoat he is staring at me and apparently has been watching my approach. I speak to her when she speaks to me and nod to him. I am prepared to go on past when suddenly she lifts her head and says on a cloud of breath: "It doesn't get this cold even in Nashville, Tennessee, does it?"

"Nashville?" Kretzer says angrily before I can answer. "You mean Asheville." His tone is officious, his voice forced, deep, and guttural. I suspect they have been quarreling. We look at each other, Mary David and I, and know to let his correction pass uncorrected.

"You never come to our café any more," she says.

"It's too cold now to cross the park."

"You live on the other side?"

"Near the Lion," I say and point toward the Lion of Belfort.

"I've often wondered. Near the Clôture de Lilas?" she asks.

On an impulse I decide it might be wise for her to know how to find me. Ignoring the suspicion in Kretzer's eyes, I say: "I live in the hotel almost directly across from there. On Montparnasse. Above the Café Margot."

Apparently she does not believe in his paranoia yet, for she says, disarmingly, "Maybe we will find you there sometime. At the café."

I say please do and she is Southern enough to know that the lack of enthusiasm means please don't. I try to see in her face if she is trying to say more than her words. But her brown eyes are watery from the cold and her nose is red, and her freckles are standing out on her winter-white cheeks.

"Maybe we will see you there or at St. Sulpice?" There is no question that her tone is wistful and for the first time guarded. Has he tightened his grip on her elbow? Is she afraid of him? "Come see us sometime," she says. "If we're not in the café we're in my apartment."

Though I do know, I tell her I do not know where her apartment is. She asks Kretzer to give me a card with the telephone number. He reaches in his greatcoat for his wallet. He draws from it a card and presents it as if it were an invitation to a duel. He returns the wallet to his coat and draws out an object which I do not at first recognize, but as Mary David and I make small talk I see it is a long knife. He flicks the blade open and studies his nicotined nails, which he begins to scrape as if we were beneath his notice with our small talk. But then he looks up deliberately, catches my eye, and begins, without looking at the razor-sharp blade, to pare the thick square nail of his left thumb.

For some days the conversation and the sight of the long-bladed knife have naturally worried me; and I have been asking about the German who caused trouble at the American Embassy. He has, it turns out, caused trouble also at an American café off the Odéon. Few Americans will go to the café at St. Sulpice. I am not at all alone in regarding him as mad.

Since I caught sight of the look in Kretzer's eyes as he

pared his nails, I have walked past the café on St. Sulpice several times, hoping to see Mary David alone and to talk with her. But each time Kretzer was there and I passed on down to the rue Bonaparte. Today, one of the first of an early spring, I have not seen him and I have entered when she waved to me: Kretzer has gone to see a doctor this afternoon. She has persuaded him at last to go because he is having trouble sleeping. "I can hear him tossing all night." It slips out. She does not turn red but explains with a no-nonsense air: "He's run completely out of money except for some sort of little pension and I'm letting him sleep in the small bedroom I never used anyway." He eats practically nothing; but he has begun to drink too much. But only in the last month has he begun to drink so much and sleep so little.

"This is the first time I've passed when he wasn't here," I say.

"He said he'd seen you pass. He notices everything." She must recognize my discomfort at this news because she changes her tone. "He loves the Vavins. Especially Robert. They've been, until recently, very sweet to him. He helps Robert move the tables and chairs in at night and out in the morning and cleans up back of the bar and is teaching him German and English. Mama and Papa Vavin are impressed because no one has been able to interest Robert in anything except athletics before." Today, even though the weather is still cold, Robert is wearing short sleeves. He moves among the tables, his tray held high, with the grace of a football player. He is very body-conscious and body-proud. I think of Denise's diagnosis of Kretzer and his needs. "If he'd find himself a boy friend . . ."

Mary David glances at her watch. "I hope the doctor will give him some sleeping pills. He won't take tranquilizers. They're part of a communist plot to lull America to sleep. He's so nervous." She says "nervous" now, not "nuhvous."

At last I can say again what I feel I must make clear to her, the reason I have been seeking this meeting. "I think it is more than nerves."

She is prepared to listen. She studies her hands and then sits as still as a cat about to be stroked.

"Mary David, the first time we talked, I told you what I thought, what other people thought. . . . Since then I've asked a good many people, at the Embassy, at several cafés, people who know, and almost without exception . . ."

She shakes her head impatiently. She cannot bear to hear more. "He's just nervous."

"Denise said she met you together at Montparnasse, and she said he seems worse than . . ."

"Denise!" Mary David says with sudden venom. "Is she that friend of yours . . ."

"She used to be," I say, "the one in black, always . . ."

"Black hair down her back, black stretch pants . . ."

I nod.

"That slattern," she says. "But I must say she's the only Frenchwoman I've ever seen who could wear stretch pants. Why do they . . ." She shakes her head; it's not worth pursuing. I realize how tense she has become. "Denise! Back home she'd be a hillbilly!"

"Careful," I say. She knows I am from the foothills. "Anyway," I say, "it's none of my business."

"Sweetie, please don't." She looks as though she cannot bear to hear more about what people think of Kretzer. I know now she sees him as clearly as I do. She knows even if she will not admit to herself or to anyone that he is a dangerous man.

We sit watching a beautiful pair of dray horses pulling a flat of wine kegs toward the Buci market. "That's the only thing that makes me homesick. Animals. And one other thing. You know what the other thing is?" she asks.

"Watermelons in the Arab quarters?"

She shakes her head. "The Frenchmen when they say 'comment.' Sometimes they drawl it out and it sounds just like 'Come on' the way Daddy used to say it when he was going to take me with him."

She checks the sentimentality in her eyes and laughs it from her voice. "Isn't the South impossible?"

"The rest of the country seems to think so," I say.

"Oh, I'm not worried about that. Soon as it gets money all that will work itself out and it'll be as standard as the rest of the country. Marching around won't do it, alone. Money, it's going to take money." But she is as tired of saying the same old things over and over as I am. "That's where we should be this minute."

I agree, but I know that neither of us feels militant enough to go back. "Denise . . ." I begin again.

"Denise! Do you know the first word that came to my mind when I saw her?"

"Slattern," I say. It is strange how women know what type of woman will attract a man they are talking to. Denise is not slatternly at all.

"Common," Mary David says. "She's common."

"Tacky?" I ask.

"No, she's got too much style for that."

For the rest of the afternoon, until it is almost time for Kretzer to come back, we list all the people we know who are common or not, tacky or not. George Washington was common and Martha tacky; Abraham Lincoln was neither; Robert E. Lee was elegant and so is James Baldwin; Marilyn Monroe began tacky but ended up neither common nor tacky. Queen Elizabeth is tacky; Margaret Rose, not. We both agree about Lady Bird and the Duchess of Windsor. We ourselves are not, of course, common or tacky because like all good Southerners we are descended from Pocahontas through the Randolphs of Virginia. This mutual, snobbish nonsense seems, sitting here in the heart of Paris, outrageously funny to us; but gradually it becomes funnier to Mary David than it is to me and as she coughs and laughs and dries her eyes with her napkin and begins laughing all over again, I know it is a deeper anguish than homesickness that is shaking her, and making her face wet with laugh-tears. When she controls herself enough to try to see the watch on her wrist, I rise to leave and this time she does not try to stop me. She quits laughing completely and says: "Honey, thank you for coming by." I say that I have enjoyed being in this common, tacky place with her.

"Will I see you again?" she asks.

"Certainly," I say.

"Is there any way to get in touch with you?" She keeps the question light, unimportant.

"I'm still looking for a better place, but in the meantime I'm stuck here." I give her my card and write the telephone number of the hotel on it.

"Is it all right to call?"

"They try to be very good about calls," I say. "They believe they speak English there. Especially over the telephone."

"I can never get through on these phones. I was hoping you had a private one."

"The surest way is to send a note by Dmitri." I point to an old Renault taxi in which a great, mustached Russian sits nodding.

The following morning before I go out for breakfast Dmitri is there with a note from Mary David: "I do need to talk to you. I will be at the Museum of Man (Trocadero stop) all afternoon (from noon till five). Please do not go near St. Sulpice or my apartment. If you are not at the museum before five I will call you at your hotel at six.

Please do not call my apartment or the café. M.D.C."

That afternoon, at the Musée d'Homme I find Mary David, not lingering where she can easily be found, near the entrance, but on a rented stool in the Hottentot room. She is sketching, copying almost every design in the showcases, floor, ceiling, any geometrical design that can be seen in the room or from the window.

She sees me, smiles, holds up her finger to indicate "one second" before finishing a design and closing the book.

I tell her to continue if she likes. But she wants rather to show me the section on American Indians. Finally she decides she has worked enough today. Her tone is matter-of-fact; she has something important to say.

We cross the wide avenue and find a table in the sun. It is only after the waiter has left us with our drinks that she speaks. She is direct as I knew she would be. "It was a mistake to send Kretzer to a doctor. One I knew nothing about." She drinks almost half her Pernod in one avid gulp. "He came back raving. I can't find out what the doctor asked him but whatever it was it was exactly the wrong thing." She sighs and holds her mouth open as if it were parched. "I got absolutely no sleep all night."

"Which doctor? At the American Hospital?"

"He won't go near there. The Vavins suggested a neurologist who teaches at the medical school."

"They're usually good. The faculty."

"Oh, I'm sure," she says. "But he got the wrong one for him. He shouldn't have known the Vavins suggested him. He came back wishing he'd killed the doctor and before morning he had it in his head the Vavins had plotted the entire examination. Now he's got the strange idea Robert was there watching the examination and listening. There's no reasoning with him."

"But Robert was waiting on us. He was in the café. . . ."

She waves her hand impatiently. "Of course." She picks up the empty Pernod glass. "Do you mind if I have another?"

Again I wait to speak but when I do my voice surprises me with its intensity: "Have you told the Vavins?"

She has not told them. Kretzer is not serious, he can't be. I say he is. She must tell them. She does not want to disturb them. Especially since she and Kretzer have run up such a bill. Already the Vavins are beginning to be less attentive. Robert lets them sit there sometimes twenty minutes, waiting on everyone else before them. Didn't I notice yesterday? Well, she did. That much, at least, is not Kretzer's imagination. It infuriates him. He says there are other reasons Robert is ignoring us, the real reasons, but he won't tell her what they are. And now since the visit to the doctor's he talks of smashing the café to bits.

I am still puzzling about the debt at the Vavins'. "But you're selling your designs, aren't you?"

"My agent has had that thing everybody in New York is getting . . . hepatitis." She gives a brief financial account of herself. She has never really been able to live away from home on her earnings, without subsidy from her father; and now he has become a perfect bastard and has cut her checks in half, trying to get her to come back to the States. Kretzer not only earns nothing now but also spends a great deal. If he lived somewhere else she could rent his room. Or if he were a different type person she could rent the third bedroom. But he will not hear of any one else in the flat with them. The doctor yesterday took absolutely the last dollar she had. She can understand Kretzer's fury about the fee.

"Are you afraid of him?" I am wondering whether she wants to borrow money and how much I can lend.

"No," she says, "he's not mean to me." She looks very tired. "He's just nervous." I advise her to warn the Vavins and to sleep somewhere else. That, she says, would really make Kretzer mad. Truly mad.

"If you want a place to stay . . ." I am saying as I pay for the second Pernod. I leave the change on the table and she cannot look away from it until she realizes she is staring.

"Could you—" she asks. "I hate to ask . . . but can you lend me some money until the first? Ten days. I'll be quite frank, that's why I was looking for you."

I give her all the money in my wallet, about twenty dollars, and tell her I can bring her some more in five days when my own check arrives. We both are too embarrassed to go into how much she actually needs; but apparently the twenty dollars is more than she expected and the prospect of additional money in five days is more than she had dreamed of.

She says casually, "Oh, that would be wonderful." But her eyes are full of gratitude and affection and she looks at me as if she has never really seen me before. "I may have to give you my solid silver cream pitcher, honey."

We laugh and begin telling stories of impoverished old Southern ladies who have sold their chandeliers and poster beds. She knows one who sold her doorknobs and had a closet full of quilts she couldn't get to because the dealer forgot to replace them all with ordinary knobs as he had promised. We both sound a little homesick, but mainly Mary David sounds tired and, after the Pernods, sleepy. She looks at her watch and stands almost immediately. "I'm late." She seems frightened whether she admits it or not. "Honey," she says, "thank you. You don't have to go now. Finish your drink."

"Well, Miss Mary David," I say as I walk her toward the subway, "I think everything's going to be all right when you get your front room rented out to some nice working gentleman." She turns from the subway entrance to the taxi stand. "They're so depressing when they're crowded. I think I'll just take a cab." She is saving face and I am glad. She is making it clear that if you want to lend a lady money you should buy her expensive drinks in a nice part of town and send her home in a cab.

Two days later when I return before lunch to my hotel from the Right Bank, I find Dmitri the taxi driver in the lobby waiting for me. He has a message from Mary David and his mustaches bristle with excitement. The note says, in quick jerky handwriting: "Kretzer tried to stab Robert. Has damned near brained him with a Cinzano ashtray. Robert in hospital. Fractured skull. Maybe more. Please come back with driver. M.D.C."

Dmitri gives me the key which Mary David has sent with the message. All afternoon I am in and about the apartment and even when I am out I keep a watch on the entrance. Toward evening I go in and have just turned on the light in the kitchen and the gas jets on the stove for heat when I hear Mary David come in the front door. I call to her so as not to frighten her and her voice is surprisingly cheerful, almost girlish. "Honey, I'm so glad you're here." She is taking off her coat and gloves and scarf and is combing her hair with her fingers before the mirror in the hall.

At the door of the kitchen she lets her pretense of energy fall and she throws her arms around my neck and her whole body trembles against mine but she does not cry as I pat her back. "Ohhh," she says in a long wavering cry. "What a day! Those damned little snotty bureaucrats . . ." Her hair has an auburn smell just as I knew it would. "Those important little people . . ." She pushes herself out of my arms.

"They're tacky, aren't they?"

"You couldn't be more right." She goes past me as if I am a coatrack she has hung all her troubles on in passing.

"They couldn't be more tacky, even if they had Cadillacs."
She begins putting pots and skillets on the stove.

"Do you know what I did?" she asks. Again her voice
is all bright and party. "I went all the way to the store back
of the Madeleine and bought a box of three-minute hominy
grits." She turns and laughs and no one could tell she'd
spent her day in hospital wards and jails and lawyers' of-
fices. "We're going to have grits and eggs and coffee and
buttered toast! Don't you think that sounds good?"

"Grits?" I ask.

"Yes," she says. "Imagine!"

"And ham," I say. "Let me go get some ham."

"And we'll have red-eye gravy."

I want an excuse to be out for a while. All afternoon I've
been adjusting myself for long consolations, philosophical
probings, psychological speculations. But I should have
known that we are both too Southern for such immediate
directness. We have had practice in avoiding a direct glance
at violence and misfortune.

"Ham would be marvelous!" Her face is beginning to
relax. For some reason I kiss her lightly on the cheek before leaving. She surprises me by holding to me a little
longer than I expect. Even as I kiss her on the forehead,
though, she is turning away toward the stove.

While out I stop at the café which during the afternoon
was closed. Madame Vavin is at her place at the cash reg-
ister. All the neighborhood is in and out, asking about
Robert, and buying drinks to his recovery. Madame does
not notice me in the crowd and I am glad. She wears an
expression balanced exactly at that point between grief and
courage which will stimulate both sympathy and business.
Habitués of other cafés who are discovering what a pleasant café this is are being invited back.

When I return to the apartment with the ham, the table

is set and candles are burning and Mary David has changed clothes and washed her face and brushed her hair. The house is full of the odor of black coffee and from a pot on the stove comes the sound of early morning childhood: the hominy has already begun to pucker and spit. The frying pan is smoking hot for the ham, another one for the eggs already cracked in a bowl. She has the corkscrew on the table ready for me to open the Beaujolais. We raise our glasses and drink to our own thoughts. She goes to her room and brings back marguerites for a centerpiece.

"It's a marvelous store," she says as she sets the pot of grits into a larger one of boiling water. She starts the ham which sizzles furiously and then the eggs. "They even have canned okra. For gumbo."

Mary David and I drink without talking until the ham begins to smoke and pop. As she takes up the eggs and the ham, she turns from the frying pans and says: "Now I can rent my rooms."

I am not sure whether she means to me or not, but I have been thinking the same thing; and if she mentions it again after supper I will let her know I will move in. I try not to look pleased but I have always known this would happen.

"Why are you smiling?" she asks. "What are you laughing at?"

" 'Miss Mary David's Boarding House.' "

She smiles. "Wouldn't you know I'd come over here and end up taking in boarders? You think all Southerners are cursed forever with genteel poverty?"

"You know what Kipling said." I have been thinking about it during the afternoon: " 'They change their skies above them, But not their hearts that roam.' "

The muscles in her face begin to play tricks on her and I want to look away while she regains control. I realize the words apply not only to Mary David and to me, three thousand miles from the violent South, but even more to Kretzer who miles and years away from his Germany is still speaking the beloved language of his concentration camp.

When I look up from the wine glass I see that she has won the struggle. Her face is smooth, as if she'd patted each betraying muscle back into place. "Isn't that funny? That's what Daddy wrote me last week. Only he was quoting from Horace. He loves Horace: 'They change their climates not their dispositions who run beyond the sea.' "

For a while we are silent. Then, as though we had worked together every night taking up supper, we put the grits, eggs, ham, toast, and coffee on the table, and the cream in the silver pitcher, the pledge for her debt to me.

"Have you tried sherry on grits?" she asks as I hold her chair for her. "You wouldn't believe how good it is."

"I certainly wouldn't," I say. "And I have no intention of finding out." She is thinking her own thoughts and I try to bring her out of them. "You are getting either decadent or international."

"Wouldn't you know," she says, and now her voice goes flat as the delta, "I'd come over here and get myself in a mess of trouble like this."

I have been determined not to say "I told you so"; but I have been asked and a certain jealousy of Kretzer, who has sat how many nights in this chair where I am sitting, pervades me and I cannot resist. "I told you he was dangerous."

"Honey," she says in real surprise, "you didn't need to tell me anything. I told everybody from the beginning he was *nervous*."

" 'Nuhvous,' " I say. "You used to say 'nuhvous.' "

"Well, I told you he was nuhvous. Be honest. Didn't I?"

I nod agreement and look up from the grits at the flowered tile around the stove. So here we sit, I think, under a Gallic sky, in one of those ambiguous Southern relationships that will never be quite brother-sister and never quite lover.

She seems to know the nature of my musings and says: "Is it 'who run beyond the sea' or 'who roam beyond the sea'?"

Before I can say that she is mixing the two quotations she raises her hand to stop me. "Listen," she whispers.

From far off through the Paris dusk comes the cry of a street haggler on his way home. "Aaah-be shee-fon . . . aah-be shee-fon." He is begging to buy old clothes and rags, but his words are sung out on that plaintive rhythm of street merchants all over the world. It makes no difference be the cry for bones and hides or for the love of Allah. "Aaah-be shee-fon . . . aah-be shee-fon!" Mary David listens as if to the rhythm of her own blood and calls back in a voice as soft and far away as the rag merchant's own: "Shwim-pee wah-wah . . . shwim-pee wah-wah." And to her sea island chant of shrimp fresh out of water, I add my own mountain lullaby of young corn and fresh vegetables: "Roastn-ears green peas . . . rose-nears green peas!" In the candlelight with the dark sky at the windows, it is too lovely for Mary David to bear, and with the heel of her hand she brushes her cheeks dry and she sings out again in answer to the far-off ragman: "Shwimp-pee wah-wah . . . shwimp-pee wah-wah!"

HEREBY HANGS A TALE

James Hawley dreamed that he had a long tail like a monkey. It became disconcerting to the entire family and eventually to the small Southern town where they had lived —up until then—in peace with themselves and their neighbors, and on happy nodding terms with Nature and Nature's Laws.

He was in love at the time. He was in love with his own wife and had been for ten years, which naturally made some people in the town rather skeptical of him. Edith Hawley, to be truthful, could have inspired little more than a gentle drowsiness or a dull ache behind the eyes in most men, but apparently she was a disturbing and endlessly fascinating creature to James, who had lived a not exactly spectacular life. "I'm afraid to look straight at the woman for fear she'll burst out crying," his old father used to bellow about Edith, and then in a surge of radiant tenderness, "or that *I* will." She did appear that timid to everyone but James. Anyway, what happened was, in a way, bound to happen, and it was sad.

Edith woke up, she later reported, about five o'clock, just before dawn, and saw in the late, late-winter moonlight her husband standing by his bed tucking the sheets under the mattress as though he were back in the Army making up his bed for inspection.

"James," she said, not realizing that he was half asleep. "James."

"Wut?" he mumbled.

"What are you doing out of bed?"

He turned toward her and as the sleep-fog drifted from his eyes they focused with anger on her face. "What?" he asked.

"What's wrong with you?"

He gazed down at his bare feet, inspected his toenails as though they were meaningless medals, then slowly gazed about the room. "Oh," he said; nothing more, just "oh," but he was plainly disturbed. He lay back in the bed, then quickly turned over on his side.

He stayed there until dawn, smoking cigarette after cigarette until his wife could not bear a silence any longer even though she was afraid to make him talk when he was not inclined to.

"What were you doing out of bed?" she asked nervously. As long as he remained silent there was the possibility that he had planned to strangle her in her sleep. "Why were you out of bed at five in the morning?" There was a carefully restrained note of anxiety in her voice.

James inhaled slowly and blew smoke out through his nostrils in a sigh. "I dreamed I had a long tail like a monkey," he said flatly. "It had got out from under the cover and was cold. I had simply got out of bed to cover it up."

"Well," said Edith. Nothing more, just "well." For the

next few minutes she watched him lying there smoking, then she asked in a triumphant tone: "How could you have covered it up if you were out of bed?"

"I couldn't," he answered as though he had been expecting exactly that technical question from her. "So it's just as well that you woke me." He shut his eyes. "It would have been frozen off by now."

"What would?"

"The long tail," he said, as though his wife might easily be the dullest woman in the world.

"Quit talking that way. You haven't got a long tail like a monkey."

James opened his eyes and a smile for a second twitched the corner of his mouth before he began frowning again.

"James, you aren't still dreaming, are you?"

"I'm awake," he said, "wide awake."

"Well, don't go back to sleep." Edith was anxiously watching his face. "You might dream again."

"I'm awake," he said, and that was all that was said until later when he was dressing. Without looking at her, he asked, "Did you go to the fire yesterday?"

"Certainly," Edith said. She had missed only one fire since she came to the town as a bride: the Burgess Hotel burned beautifully without her because James's mother held the car keys firmly in her apron pocket saying: "That isn't the kind of place a respectable woman watches burn."

"Was it a good fire?" James asked, tying his tie.

"So-so," she reported. All fires were so-so to Edith even though she could not easily be kept away from them, and even though when she watched them a tiny gleam of life, almost akin to joy, came into her usually expressionless face. "Sometimes when she watches a fire and the firemen her little gray eyes almost dance," James used to brag, and it must have been at such times that he found her especially bewitching, mysterious, and alive.

"Was Scala there?" he asked.

"Scala?"

"The fire chief."

"Yes," Edith yawned. "He carried the hose up the ladder. I think that was Scala."

James turned quickly, and if Edith had been more observant she might have seen jealousy drain the color from his face and the strength from his body. He sat down heavily, then stood up quickly and glanced in the mirror at the seat of his pants. He was still studying himself when Edith asked: "Why don't you be a fireman?"

Color, in fact one color after another, came back into James's face. "LOCAL BANK TELLER BECOMES FIREMAN TO PLEASE WIFE," he read from a sensational, imaginary newspaper. He was furious. "You can't make a monkey out of . . ." He stopped suddenly and brushed at the seat of his trousers. His voice was cool, almost humble when he spoke again: "Why don't you marry Scala?"

"Whatever for?" Edith asked.

"You seem to like men who climb around with long . . ."

Edith interrupted, which she had never done before. "Just because I like fires and crowds and excitement! Back home in Louisville, I went to the races every year"—her voice was threatening to rise a note above its usual level— "but I didn't marry Man-o'-War." She had made a joke! Her mouth remained open in what might have been amazement. She moved to the mirror and looked at the creature who had made a joke. She almost smiled at her image.

"See," James said, desperately, "you are changing."

He put his arms around her. "And I don't want you to change. Ever."

"You're the one who's changing," she said.

James turned red and hurried from the room.

"We just won't mention it, not even to the preacher," old

Mrs. Hawley said when Edith came downstairs that morning to tell her how James had dreamed about having a long tail, how he had tried to cover it up, and how later he had rushed from the room. Old Mr. Hawley was delighted. As far back as he could remember no Hawley he had ever heard of had had a long tail like a monkey.

"Well certainly no one on my side of the family ever had," Edith said in utter confusedness, but perhaps in the mild hope of escaping responsibility.

"What kind of family did I marry into?" old Mrs. Hawley cleared herself with innocence and dignity.

"My, my." James's father was grinning proudly. "A long tail."

They talked about James all morning. They agreed that he had always seemed excessively conservative, modest, and, in nice words, dull. He was and had always been, even as a boy, a gentleman. This growing a long tail was very unlike him. The two women speculated on his embarrassment, and after persuading old Mr. Hawley with threats, they all agreed that no word would be spoken about the tail either in the house or out. Old Hawley must not, above all things, brag.

Edith had not reported the conversation about the fires. She had been careful not to mention Scala, the chief. She could not imagine how James had found out about her secret crush on the fireman, except perhaps by the fact that she had missed only one fire in ten years. She merely said, "I'm glad we aren't going to talk about it any more."

They were indeed innocent, though, if they thought silence would cure James. During the weeks that followed they were forced through their agreement to ignore his new habits. He would not wear his thin overcoat because it did not have a split back. He began walking through doors backward or else turning completely around before shutting them cautiously and gently. He would not let anyone walk behind him, and on the few occasions when there were visitors he either stood with his back to the wall, or perched painfully on the edge of a chair. During the second week he abandoned his usual overstuffed chair in favor of a Windsor. His parents glanced quickly at each other with worried and baffled expressions. His father finally found an excuse to walk behind the Windsor where James sat. He stared suspiciously at it and at the floor.

Finally Edith had to speak. "Why have you changed chairs?"

James again blushed. He cleared his throat and spoke: "I'm tired of that one. Just thought I'd try out this."

Edith stared at the open back of the Windsor chair and at the distance between the spindles. "Don't you think . . ." Then she stopped. There was no use worrying him with the idea that it might get stuck between the spindles; he would have to sit somewhere. A standing man in the house would make her nervous.

"Think what?" he asked.

"Think," she paused, "you might sit in your own chair if you sit kind of sideways."

"Possibly," he said with somewhat injured dignity. "But I see no reason to contort myself into a spectacle." He stood up, strode bravely from the room, then turned shyly around to keep from shutting the door on himself.

Old Mrs. Hawley glared at Edith, who gazed back with her face, as usual, expressionless.

That was as near as they came to speaking openly about James's condition. He himself, though, tiptoed near the subject one night at supper when he refused a piece of chocolate cake.

"It used to be your favorite," his mother said.

"I'm tired of it," he said, "there are other kinds of cake, you know."

"What kind would you like?"

"Any kind. Coconut."

Perhaps they would not have thought anything about his new preference except that he turned red and redder. His father's eyes were sparkling with pride and twice he opened his mouth to ask James a question, but each time his mother coughed.

However successful the family was in hiding its concern and interest in James's behavior, the clerks, officials, and clients of the Chate Street Bank did not know exactly how to react to a series of sudden changes in his activities. They first noticed that he locked the gate behind him when he walked into his cage in the morning, so that the ease and cooperativeness which the tellers had enjoyed among themselves were ended. His old customers saw that he no longer smiled at them when reaching for their deposits and in fact that he seemed to grab and rake in the money as though he were acquiring personal property to be hidden carefully away.

All of this was whispered about, but no one said anything openly until James began eating peanuts during the slack hour and throwing the shells on the floor. First the janitor complained and then the cashiers in the adjoining cages. James was not too careful about where he threw the shells. When asked about his new diet, which apparently now required six hours of steady munching, he said, "I've got to keep healthy." And if no clients were in the bank he would open the gate and swing and chin himself on the overhead crossbar. The bank president, who was forced by a cashier to watch my uncle from his balcony office, merely said that when men start approaching middle age they sometimes begin worrying about their health and strength. He had a great deal of faith in James.

James Hawley, though, was losing faith in himself. When warm weather came the bank installed its revolving doors. Sometimes my uncle would stand for five or ten minutes before going through them. He would emerge white and shaken on the other side. After the ordeal of coming through the doors each morning he perched moodily on his high stool until the first customer appeared at the window of his cage. That brought him out of his despair and for the remainder of the open-day he rushed about the cage in furious activity: reaching out and grabbing money and deposit books from clients, throwing back deposit slips or money to them, rarely speaking. No one suspected that he had a long tail.

One Tuesday morning in May, however, Goodman's furniture store, three blocks from the bank, rang a fire alarm. James was out of his cage and through the doors before anyone could swear they had seen him leave. When he returned forty minutes later he was carrying a sixteen-pound bag and was such a pitiful sight that the president came down to ask him if anyone was hurt or killed in the fire.

"Just me," James said.

The president laughed and went back up to his balcony.

When the president looked back down again, James had not reopened his window, which had been closed during his absence. He was eating bananas out of the large bag, tossing the peels on the floor of his own cage and the adjoining one. Two peels were hanging on the grillwork above his window. It was at that unfortunate moment that Mother Osborne approached the window to deposit $16.25, the sum total of a penny collection which her Sunday school had conducted.

"Mr. Hawley, I know you're a good man . . ." She never finished the sentence. The words enraged James. He seized the bars and shook them with such vigor that the grillwork rattled around the entire bank lobby. Mother Osborne dropped the paper sack of pennies and retreated through the rolling pennies, across the bank, then turned and fled through the door.

James did not tell the family that he had been fired, or as the president said: "Relieved of duties until you have had sufficient rest to regain your composure." Instead, he sat without eating at the supper table and stared at Edith, who chewed steadily and constantly, pausing only at set intervals to sip lukewarm water. When she at last glanced away from her plate long enough to see him staring at her, she almost dropped a forkful of rice; but recovered it in time to continue the unbroken rhythm of her chewing.

"How did you like the fire?" James asked quietly.

"So-so," Edith answered.

"Did you have to applaud Scala before everybody in town?" James asked her later when they were upstairs alone.

"Everybody clapped," she said.

"No," he shook his head sadly. "You were the only one."

"Well, they should have. That was a magnificent leap. When a man jumps five feet from the top of one building to another, people ought to cheer."

"You did your part," James said.

"I didn't see you there. Why weren't you sitting safely in your bank?"

"I can do other things too," James answered. He walked to the window and stared out at a giant oak, its tender new leaves fluttering softly. "Five feet isn't far to jump."

The next morning James left the house at seven forty-five, as though he were on his day to work at the bank. By ten o'clock, however, the family knew he had been fired. Naturally the news was all over town. The way many people heard and told the story—and still do, for that matter—was that James threw banana peels in Mother Osborne's

face, jumped through the window, snatched a $60.25 bag
of money from her, ran out, and was caught at the Goodman fire. Another story spread that he had set fire to the
furniture store, and another that Scala had jumped across
a five-foot chasm to capture James on the roof of the next
building. Everyone was talking about the Chate Street
Bank robbery even though the switchboard operators both
there and at the newspaper office were denying that even
a penny had been lost or stolen. A department store man-
ager phoned old Mrs. Hawley to ask her to see a display of
mink coats an agent was showing in his office, and an automobile dealer tried to sell Edith a yellow convertible. No
one could find James Hawley.

"You stay here. I don't want you swaggering all over
town today," his mother said at lunch to her husband.
"Edith, you stay here and see that he doesn't leave. I'm
going out to find James."

It was late that afternoon when she found him in the
Zoo Park. He was standing in front of the moat at the
Monkey Mountain. A spider monkey leapt from a rock to
the limb of a young poplar, caught with one hand, and
swung by its tail. James laughed out with delight. "How far
would you say that was?" he asked, as though he knew
without turning that his mother was standing behind him.

"Five feet," she said.

"Oh, it's more than that. It must be twelve. Ten anyway."

Another monkey jumped and swung by his tail. James
clapped and cheered. An old man and woman who had
been tossing peanuts over the moat watched him, then
edged away, whispering to each other. A little redheaded
boy called to a monkey and threw it the last of his popcorn.
James took a bag of peanuts out of his pocket, selected two
large ones, and ate them.

His mother held out her hand for the peanuts. He put the

bag in his pocket without glancing away from the monkeys. "You'll ruin your supper," she said.

"Did you make banana pudding?" he asked.

"I will," she said. She glanced shyly at the old woman who had begun edging back closer to listen. "Come on, James, let's go home."

"All right," he said as though that were a wonderful idea, but as she led him away he was stumbling along, staring back over his shoulders at the swinging monkeys. He stopped in front of Maggie's cage and handed the ugly baboon the bag of peanuts while his mother looked on jealously. He glanced back once more at the swinging monkeys. "I don't see how they do it." He sighed. "I'm tired, just from studying them." As they drove home there was chill in the air and gray in the sunset.

His mother stole glimpses of him from the corner of her eyes and drove on in silence. She followed him from the garage and stopped when he did under the oak in the back yard. "How far would you say that straight limb is from the gable?" He pointed to the peaked roof over his bedroom window.

"Ten or fifteen feet," she said.

"That far?"

"Why?" she asked.

He stood as though he were holding the door open for her but she had to open it for herself. "No reason," he said. "Wondering, wondering, wondering."

For supper James ate a whole banana pudding. A dreadful silence was in the dining room. He pushed back his chair and went up the steps. The family listened to his soft footsteps on the stairs. Suddenly there were running steps, a door slammed shut, and a key clicked in the lock. Edith hurried up the steps. "James! James! What are you going to do?"

There was no answer.

"James." She rapped on the door. "James, what are you going to do?"

"Something Scala can't," he answered. He dropped one shoe to the floor, then the other. "If he can jump five, I can jump ten. He can't make a monkey out of me. Not while *I'm* alive."

"He's going to jump," old Mrs. Hawley gasped from the landing. She ran down the steps to the telephone and dialed furiously. "Hello hello yes Scala Mr. Scala this is Mrs. Hawley James is jumping out the window bring a ladder bring a net don't make any noise hurry hurry."

Old Mr. Hawley and Edith followed her into the yard. Sure enough, through the thickening dusk they could make out James climbing out of the dormer window of his bedroom. Slowly he crawled up the roof and out onto the gable. There he sat down and with great care began taking off his shirt and undershirt. He folded them neatly, and placed them beside him.

"Sh-h," his mother whispered, when Edith started to call out.

He took off his socks, placed the toes together and rolled them into a ball. Darkness was closing over the housetop, but when he stood up they could see him against the blackening gray sky. He took off his trousers, held them upside down by the cuffs, and stretched them out on the roof. In his white shorts, hands on hips, he did fourteen knee-bends. His knees creaked each time.

"Listen," his father said, "he's not in good shape for jumping. Lucky he's got a long tail to catch by."

James must have been worried by the creaking too. He tried a few more knee-bends then proceeded to waist-bends.

"Why aren't they here? Why isn't Scala here?" His mother whispered to herself and to the black sky.

"Scala!" Edith said. "No. He musn't come here. He

mustn't stop him. We've got to let him jump." She paused. In the distance the fire truck was chugging up the hill, sounding, without a siren or bell, more like a water wagon or moving van. On the roof James paused in his warming-up exercises. When he quit moving his white shorts disappeared in the darkness. Even the gray stone chimneys were invisible against the black sky. His mother squeezed Edith's arm. "Where is he? Where? Can you see him?"

Without warning Edith screamed. "Jump, James! You can make it!"

"No! Don't, don't!" his mother hollered.

"Jump. Scala is coming with a net. Jump, James, jump!"

"Catch with your hands too," old Mr. Hawley bellowed. "Just in case."

Hollow footsteps rushed across the rooftop and were drowned out by his mother's screams, his father's cheers, and the fire truck's bell as it swung, with a blinding light, into the drive.

"James!" Edith yelled. "James! Did you jump?"

"He must have run over the rooftop," his father said, after searching the ground for something apparently the size of a butter pat. "He's hiding on the front roof."

"Up on the roof. Up there, quick," his mother shouted to the firemen who were unhooking the ladder. Scala began climbing even as the ladder shot skyward. He and three other firemen searched the roof with their flashlights.

"He's not up here," Scala called. He shone the light down the chimney well. "Or down here."

"He was going to jump to the oak," old man Hawley hollered.

Scala flicked the tree briefly with the light beam. "No human being could jump that far." He shone the light down at the father. "I've jumped all my life and I wouldn't dare risk a leap like that."

"But you don't have . . ." old Mr. Hawley began.

Old Mrs. Hawley interrupted: "Mr. Scala, would you mind directing your light to the tree."

"No'm. But I tell you, it's impossible . . ."

"There!" old Mrs. Hawley called.

The spot of light danced, held still.

There, hanging by one elbow and one knee, James was struggling feebly to climb up on the limb.

"He did it. He did it." Old man Hawley danced in the drive.

"But he had to use his hands too," his mother said, in an effort to calm her husband.

"Wait, we'll get a ladder," Scala called, climbing down from the roof.

"You will not," Edith said. "My husband can take care of himself."

James's tree-climbing was not as professional as his jumping. Slowly, almost motionless at times, he climbed down the trunk in the strong spotlight from the fire truck. Edith was waiting for him. She brushed the bark dust from his chest, then placed her cheek there as she hugged him around the waist.

"Are you hurt?" his mother asked, seeing the thin streams of blood along the tiny scratches on his face and shoulders.

"Just my tail," James answered, his arm around Edith.

"What happened to it?" his father asked.

"It broke off, at the base."

"Oh." His father shook his head. "That's a shame."

"Should we call a doctor?" his mother asked.

"No," James said, his breath at last coming back to him in long heavy gasps. "I won't be needing it again."

Together, arms about each other, he and Edith walked to the back steps while Scala stood in the drive and flashed the light from the housetop to the oak limb. "Say, you!

Wait a minute," Scala called. "Do you want a job as a fireman?"

Edith looked back over her shoulder and said coldly: "Why should my husband want to be a fireman? He's a banker."

James held the door open for his wife. He followed her in and let the door bang shut behind him—without turning around.

HEAR THE WIND BLOW

When the early hunters, Boone and those before him, were exploring the Blue Ridge and the Smokies, Eaglenest Valley was plainly marked on every penciled map and homemade chart, for even though the animal paths and Indian trails rarely led down into the bowl, the hunters themselves recognized the place with sharp wonder and delight. "Pushing forward from the North, there on your left you will see it—a little lake of cloud or fog, soft as bird down." "The third day, gaining the ridge, we looked down into a nest of angel hair." Perhaps because it was vulnerable to Cherokee attack—there being no pass for rescue or retreat, no road for heavy wagons—the valley was late being peopled.

Today it is no longer marked on any ordinary road map. The nearest highway is forty miles away, and when, as sel-

136

dom happens, a native has need of a new plow or a bolt of denim, he climbs the mountain ring by mule or afoot and makes his way by boat down to Troy Town on the Hickory Styx river.

Here in the valley the weather is not akin to that outside the ring of mountains. Often, for instance, the valley will be cool as fern dew while the surrounding country will be stone dry and like a hearth. One must admit that usually the difference is in favor of the valley people. They themselves insist to the rare visitor that this place has the mildest summers, the warmest winters, and during crop-season the most luxurious rains, glorious suns, and later the luckiest of harvest moons. Reluctantly they gaze at a lone chimney on the mountainside.

A black ring round the chimney marks roughly the dimensions of the Marrow house. Elixir weed and hope vine, honeysuckle, and tares are creeping in now from the scrub pine woods to cover the charred soil and smoke-sooted rocks, but when Miranda and Thomas Marrow lived here the yard was raked clean and bare, and speckled chickens took dust baths in the fine white sand that before the wedding Thomas had brought up from the fern dell.

The one-room house had been built of squared logs by Thomas Marrow's grandfather and had been rechinked with clay, once by his father and once by himself. A lean-to of pine slabs had been added across the back in which to store potatoes, cotton, tobacco and the few unseasonal clothes. In this room ears of purple and yellow popcorn, strings of peppers, bay leaf, sassafras root, and rabbit skins hung from the low rafters. A pen in the corner held the baby pigs and lambs if wolves were about. Here in winter the speckled chickens roosted.

Through the two front windows and front door of the log house Miranda and Thomas could see only the valley floor.

At sunrise or sundown or at changes in the weather they were obliged to stand in their open yard to observe the sky above the rim of mountaintops.

"White sand would be nice here," Miranda had said during their engagement. She had stamped her brogans on the frozen red earth while surveying the house where Thomas wanted her to live. The next day Thomas had hauled up the sand, for he was an aging man, past forty, with only a house and thirty-two acres to offer and she was fifteen and sensible and that year the only child of marrying age in the whole valley. When she saw the sand and the way he had scrubbed the cabin floor with lye-drippings she said: "We maybe ought to have the wedding while everything is so clean and new-like." Thomas ran about the valley like a fly-bitten colt, his old bald head disappearing into every window and door asking all the kin and neighbors—who truth to tell were also kin—to the wedding. In a week it was done and Miranda had raked the footprints of the last guests from the white sand and settled down as pretty and calmly as a wood dove.

For Thomas it was not so easy. That spring he could not stay working the tobacco and tomato slips for running back to the house, or whistling up until she would appear on the porch and wave, or for going off to find a rubyrock for her mantelpiece collection. The valley folks winked and were secretly proud of what a fool Thomas was making of himself: he had always been so pent-up and close-mouthed while taking care of old Will Marrow and Mamie till their deaths two weeks apart, four years eight months before.

Summer came early that year. The bottomland corn was higher than the mule ears and rustled thickly, a luxurious, arousing sound to Thomas, like the frou-frou of taffeta petticoats. Rain swept over the valley in gusts, sashaying across the sanded yard in a tantalizing waltz and folding and unfolding in sheets across the split oak shingles. The oak tree

creaked in rhythm and Thomas sitting near the hearth red-
dened as he looked out across the bed at the summerwet
valley.

August, though, turned up dry. The corn wilted. The pas-
ture grass parched, the tobacco leaves curled dry, and the
green vegetables were burned to the stalks. The harvest
which in June had seemed so certainly plentiful was scant
enough to strike fear into the craws of the old who remembered other hungry years. There would be some grain for
the chickens, perhaps enough to keep the cattle alive, but
certainly not enough to fatten the razor-backs. Hog-killing
was like a funeral. Each day the valley folks looked out
across the stony mountains at the slated sky and then meas-
ured the lowering well water and watched the springs bub-
ble low and die. All night dust-devils danced over the bottomland and in the valley road. Nowhere was there the
sound of running water.

That autumn Miranda, sick each dawn with her first full-
ness, stood on the porch and watched the fog-sheep grazing
on the parched hillside and the wolf-clouds sneaking over
the mountains into the sky and was cold with fear. Shiver-
ing, she would crawl under the quilt at Thomas's side and
whisper: "Everything will be all right, won't it?"

"We will pray that it will," Thomas would whisper, for
he was a thoroughly religious, simple, straightforward, and
practical man, and the thing he wanted most then in all this
world was a son, well-born and strong. It happened often in
the valley, where all were kin to some degree, that a child
would be born puny and would die the same day. Now
though that he had a bearing wife, Thomas wanted more
than just an ordinary son: he wanted a son who would be a
saint. "We must be careful what we say and think and do.
We must begin already so that he will be honest." Miranda,
who had no special concern at first for anything except the
physical perfection of the child and her safe deliverance,

began to pray with Thomas that their souls be without ran-
cor during this time and that the child be an example of
their love. "One good man, without hate," Thomas said,
"could change the valley folk." Truth to tell, the valley folk
were no worse than any others, but being cooped up together and living slower they had a better chance to study
carefully the sins of their neighbors. Nevertheless, the first
thing in the morning, before breakfast, Thomas and Miranda prayed; again at noon, and in the evening they read
the Bible and explained it to each other and pondered
goodness and its possible effect in the wicked valley.

Miranda, who had a strong back and great natural dignity, carried herself well and though the neighbors knew
she was pregnant they were so concerned with the need of
water they had no idea how near her time was. Late in December, near four o'clock one windy day, Thomas knocked
at old Huldah Broodkey's door and announced: "It's Miranda's time. Come quick." Huldah grabbed her bag made
of red carpet, her shawl, her pipe, a twist of tobacco and at
a hobble followed the running man to the log house. He
was kneeling by the bedside praying when old Huldah,
panting, entered. Huldah stared at him with her one good
eye, letting the other drooping lid sag even more, while
she thumbed the tobacco and filled her pipe. When it
was drawing properly, she kicked Thomas's butt with the
toe of her boot and said: "Git."

He got. He went first down to the spring and regarded
how low the water bubbled. He took the bucket from the
hickory tree and finally managed to fill it half full. He returned to the house and set the bucket gently on the porch,
handy to the door. He went down again to the spring and
followed the trickle of water down the creek bed to the
wide sandy hollow. Here where the ferns were drybrown
and curled, he began filling a hod with sand which he
carried back to the cabin and emptied in the yard. He en-

visioned Miranda's delight when she should see the yard a foot thick in new sand.

At dark he stopped his work and asked Huldah's permission to come into the house and warm for a moment at the fire. Miranda was asleep. While Huldah fried a hoe cake of corn bread on the hearth coals and set out a slab of ham and a mug of hot liquor, Thomas gazed with wide eyes about the room as though he had never seen it before. Huldah had done all the necessary things: the knife was under the bed to cut the pain, the feathers had been burned to protect the child from evil outside the valley, and the Bible had been allowed to fall open and the page and ink-spotted verse noted. Occasionally Miranda tossed and moaned in her sleep, but Huldah ignored her while they ate the smoked ham and buttered corn bread. Lighting her pipe again, Huldah watched the sputtering fire logs and cackled softly.

"It was a December day just like this when I delivered that Foodleberry baby." Thomas knew of the child that had been born with its brains outside of its head, but he knew he could not stop Huldah's long, lurid descriptions. Huldah had been known to make strong men faint with her medical tales and she had a special gift for punishing fathers for siring children. No one questioned her right to torture the men during the hours their women lay in labor.

She talked for hours in a whispering monotone, never realizing that Thomas was muffling her speech with prayers of his own. She suspected once, in talking about the Treadwater baby who never grew a backbone, that Thomas was asleep. She insisted that he roll another log on the dying coals while she described the Whittummy boy who had been born looking like a watershrunk rat and had died of old age before he was seven months old. "Did you ever see a body with no eyes? Just solid bone where its eye-sockets ought to be? Thirty years ago . . ." she began another, but Thomas was asleep and Miranda was breathing in gasps. Huldah knocked out the pipe on the heel of her hand and moved quietly to the bedside.

It was pink dawn when Thomas awoke. During his sleep he had dreamed of rain and then he had dreamed of boy babies and girl babies and once of a cherub. But he had not seen them nor heard them cry. Old Huldah sat nodding before the roaring fire and Miranda lay smiling asleep with the covers tucked gently about her chin. Thomas sat shaken with wonder. He moved slowly, bent forward, and touched old Huldah's knee, lightly, lest she cry out in alarm. Huldah opened her good eye, shut her mouth and inclined her head to listen to Thomas's question: "Is it a girl or a boy?"

"It's an egg!" Huldah said.

For a moment the drooped eyelid raised and Thomas looked into the profound hollow of its socket.

"Huldah," he managed, "I don't give in to fainting spells."

"Nobody's asking you to faint." Huldah's voice was low, insistent. "It's an egg."

Maybe, Thomas thought, this is a trick Huldah plays on all the fathers. She probably has a big egg that she places in the bed and she hides the baby elsewheres. He tiptoed to the lean-to and peered into the gloom for sight of a hidden baby. Only the popcorn and peppers hung from the rafters.

"Shut the door," Huldah ordered. "You'll freeze us out."

Thomas shut the door, came back to the fire. His solemn, leathery face tried to wrinkle into a smile. "What have you done with him?"

Huldah with hand and stick pushed herself out of the chair and hobbled over to the bed. Softly she lifted the star-meadow quilt and turned back the covers to reveal a large egg, which Miranda in her sleep was nestling close to her side within the gentle curve of her arm. An intense delight came into Thomas's eyes and an immediate fatherly love into his voice: "May I lift it?"

Huldah shook her head. "No. Wait."

She covered it again, ignoring Thomas's protesting hand.

"Wait," he said. "What color is it?" He bent low to peep.

"Blue," Huldah answered. "Blue. At first I was thinking it would be speckled, but those were just blood flecks that wiped away."

"My goodness!" Thomas said, for no one in the valley within his memory had ever given birth to an egg. "How much does it weigh?"

"Nigh on to eight pounds, I'd reckon."

Thomas breathed deeply and with growing pride asked: "Have you ever seen such a fine big egg?"

Huldah said that she never in her life had.

Miranda stirred peacefully and seemingly a light breeze moved across her brow and opened her eyes and cleared the mist of sleep from them. She gazed deeply into Thomas's face and then appeared to remember him and their life together. Without moving her head she let her eyes turn slowly to regard the egg. A smile came to her lips and eyes and to her pain-hoarse voice: "It's sky blue, Thomas." For in truth the egg was light in tint.

"Like yours," he said, regarding her eyes.

"And yours," she assured him.

"Like everybody's in the valley," Huldah said flatly. She had a way of exploring all resemblances between newborns and every conceivable male in the valley. "More the color, I'd say, of Tad Walker's." Now Tad Walker was thought of in those parts as a cuckoo bird which let others bring up his young and the mention of his name at a cradleside was enough to infuriate any young father. But Thomas was forty, proud, and love-wise. He recognized his rightful own and no one could cast doubts upon it.

Miranda however objected and argued: "But Tad Walker's got such a low forehead." She stroked the smooth egg with complete assurance and pride.

They watched Huldah tap her pipe against the heel of her hand and listened to her giddy, insinuating humming, and watched her hobble down toward the bottomland road along which she would no doubt confide that Tad Walker had been up to his old pranks. But before she had vanished into the dusty rhododendron, Thomas and Miranda had pushed her out of their minds and were again smiling fondly at the egg as though it were not the baldest, blankest, barest, nakedest thing in the world.

"Do you think maybe it's cold?" Thomas asked.

Miranda felt the egg and let her palm rest on its smooth surface. "It doesn't feel cold. Still it wouldn't hurt to wrap it up a bit."

She directed Thomas to the small maple box from which he pulled out a knitted pink shawl and a pink cap with a silk ribbon. "Just the shawl," Miranda said, and if she were embarrassed by sight of the pitifully small cap, the ribbon of which would not reach around the egg in any direction, she did not show it. She simply said: "The cap is away too small."

"He's a fine big head," Thomas announced, and with some awkwardness he placed the cap carefully back into the box which held the few baby clothes Miranda had crocheted during the hot, dry months.

Whatever old Huldah had whispered did not persuade the valley folks. They filed in and out all afternoon; and not one of them suggested by smile or word or nod or wink that the egg looked like Tad Walker. True, at first they didn't know exactly what to say or how to act or whether to ask to be allowed to hold it or to kiss it. Finally words came to them.

"From here up," Miss Perryable said, with hand saluting the bridge of her nose, "it looks just like Thomas."

The others studied Thomas's bald head and agreed oh that it did indeed.

Some of them merely said my my.

And some of the older ones said well they never in all their lives, for of course they never had.

And one withered, kind lady said, "Miranda, you're the clever one!"

They nodded their heads and retreated as fast as politely possible to the sand yard where they clucked their tongues and wagged their noggins and by talking explained to themselves how such a thing had occurred so close to home. "It's all this dry weather," Miss Perryable had suggested. From that they developed the idea which old Huldah summed up and announced for them in a firm, authoritative, indisputable tone: "It's a calcified caul."

Satisfied, warmer about their hearts and colder in their feet, they stamped their way home to sit before their drowsy fires and marvel awhile: puzzled and perplexed, secretly frightened by the silent egg.

Deep within the dark hollow of night, Thomas and Miranda, curled about the egg, were awake after dreamful sleep. In their breathing was a sobbing and each listened in pain to the other's sorrow. In the lean-to a young lamb bleated, lost, and was silent.

"Thomas," Miranda whispered, finding his hand and curving it around her neck. "Why has this happened to us?"

Thomas, as though he had been explaining to himself in the darkness, answered. "Maybe we didn't pray enough?"

"Maybe"—Miranda's voice was frosted with bitterness —"we prayed too much."

"And all we wanted," Thomas continued, like a whipped child explaining to himself, "was a strong baby who we could teach to love everybody."

"I wanted a little boy people couldn't help picking up and asking: 'Whose angel child are you?' "

"And we'd be proud to say," Thomas said, his arm about the egg, " 'He's our angel child!' "

"Thomas!" Miranda was suddenly filled with joy. "Angels have wings!" Her whisper echoed in the cabin. "Do you reckon?"

After a long silence Thomas spoke in rebuke: "No, Miranda. You musn't hanker for miracles. We got to accept what is given us, without hope."

But between them the egg seemed enormous.

Together they tented the covers to peep under. In the window's slanted light the egg seemed to them to be glowing, as though throbbing with a secret light, a moon within. Miranda and Thomas shut their eyes, dazed, and pipped their lips in breathless, voiceless prayer: "Give us the strength to keep it warm."

In the valley the night had been restless. Solitary faces had peered from the windows at the light in the cabin. The Stenhouse cow had bawled all night and at dawn had dropped a dead calf and herself had fallen dead. Twenty people stood at the moment near the Stenhouse barn, glancing from time to time at the smoke boiling up from the cabin chimney.

"A light all night," Miss Perryable said without shame. No one would suspect now that she had once secretly hoped to marry Thomas herself.

"And all that smoke."

"No ordinary fire."

"My chickens," Stenhouse declared, "didn't fly down from the oak till I threw a rock." People listened with respect to the new dignity in his voice: his cow lay dead. "All this dry weather we should have suspected wasn't natural."

"If you ask me," Miss Perryable stated in a voice which reminded them that they certainly should have asked her, "the dry weather didn't cause the caul. It caused the dry weather!"

"Ah so!" they said.

They were tired of drought, tired of dust and coughing, tired of measuring water and studying a slated, cloudless sky. They were tired of shouting down dry wells.

"I've nothing against Tom and Miranda!" an ancient man sagely announced as though only the experience and tolerance and wisdom of old age prevented him from having. He grated his gnarled hands together and squinted his eyes until they were sewed shut with brier stitches of laugh wrinkles.

"Grandpa," Miss Perryable said, "I've never known of you doing or saying one mean thing." She always flattered him to hide her suspicion: she did not in the least believe he was a hundred and three years old. It was doubly wise to speak kindly to him now. "You couldn't hate anyone without *good* reason."

The pale valley eyes searched the creases in the old man's face. He spoke in a whimper: "My bunions ache and I can't soak them."

"Poor Grandpa," the withered, kind lady said.

"I've nothing against Tom and Miranda either," Stenhouse said. He gazed toward the barn where the poor little old calf had been born dead. "Nothing against Miranda leastwise."

"She was sweet," a woman in a bonnet said, "when she was a baby."

"Such a shaming pity. And her with her ma dead."

No one was fooled by these words. They all knew what Miranda's mother had done: she had once worn an apron to church under her dress because she'd been too lazy to wash out a petticoat. That was the truth, there were those who knew for a fact.

"Perhaps we best leave her ma out."

They nodded gravely.

Since soon after sunrise Thomas with his broken-handled ax had been up on the ridge cutting a dead hickory tree, and Miranda had been propped up in bed sewing rabbit skins into a square blanket. A fire roared in the chimney and the cabin creaked with heat. Toward noon old Huldah came pushing through the rhododendron. She halted at sight of the smoke from the cabin chimney and regarded Thomas with his ax. "Brooding ain't easy!" she cackled. She hobbled up the steps, with Thomas behind, ready to catch her did the sticks give way. Inside, Huldah cackled again. "Hot enough to hatch a buzzard!"

Thomas clenched his fists around the ax handle. But when Miranda nodded her head gently, Thomas relaxed and grinned. "What are you doing up here prying around already?"

Huldah wheeled about on her sticks. "Man, I'm not prying. I know more than I want to know and suspect the rest."

Thomas pushed forward the chair.

"I can't sit. Cause I got trouble. And you got trouble. I come to warn you. The folks is getting themselves all worked up over this egg. You best git." She started toward the door, but Thomas stood in her way. "Let me out, Tom Marrow, I got to be back before they miss me gone."

"How worked up? About what?"

"They ain't understanding this. I say git till they do."

"What would you say, Huldah, did a child break through that shell? What would the folks down there say?"

"If anything comes out of that shell, it'll have to have feathers." Huldah was delighted. "And they'll be needing only tar to finish the job they got in mind."

"And what if it turns out to be an angel child?"

"Oh man!" Huldah hooted. "You've done taken leave of

your sense. Just cause they got wings don't mean they come out of eggs." She pushed past Thomas and hitched herself down the steps. "Wait till they hear this!"

As the old woman poked her way into the rhododendron, Miranda, watching, cried. "But we can't leave. How would we live? How would we keep him warm?"

"We aren't leaving." Thomas spoke with angry determination. "It's only old Huldah with her tales. She likes to be aggravating." He walked to the door and glared down at the road. "The folks down there will talk like they always do when they're puzzled or scared, but they won't try nothing."

During the afternoon he cut arm-length pieces of wood and tossed them into a pile. Between the ax-swings he would sometimes pause to stare down into the valley. But when the steady rhythm of the chopping was broken, Miranda would call out, frightened: "Thomas!" He would call back: "I'm merely resting a bit." Late in the afternoon the pauses became more frequent as he watched the people, no larger from here than field mice, running frantically about the bottomland road, gathering in groups and dispersing. When curious shouts came up from below he chopped even faster to hide the sounds from Miranda. Each time he would go into the cabin he would carry an armload of wood and stack it on the hearth against the chimney. By dark there were two stacks that reached to the mantelpiece where in the lamplight Miranda's rubyrocks sparkled like fresh blood.

The fire was blasting in the chimney and the cabin was so dry hot that with parched lips Miranda begged him to leave the door ajar. In the doorlight he continued cutting logs until the porch had a banister of wood stacked three feet high. By moonup at seven they were both tired past speaking. The wood cut, the rabbit-fur blanket finished, the egg would brood warm. Body-numb they sat on the bed and waited, dozed and waited, nodded, slept, woke, and waited. Sitting upright, their heads fell forward. They slept exhausted.

Suddenly wide awake they jumped and sat shaking. The crash still sounded in their ears.

"Did you hear that?"

"What was it?"

They were both feeling the warm hollow of the bed. The egg was still there nestled safely.

"A gunshot."

"Or a window breaking."

Another rock landed on the oak roof. Pebbles rained against the cabin. Angry shouts pierced the night.

Thomas leaned forward and peered out the window. In the midnight moonlight dark shadows struggled up the path dragging a burning tree. At the edge of darkness, on the white sand, two tense silhouettes danced Indian dances—bending over, gathering stones, hurling them at the cabin. "Hell fire, hell fire," they seemed to be shouting in a noise like laughter, or, "Well dry, well dry."

"Thomas," Miranda whimpered.

"Shhh," he calmed her. "It's only the valley folks."

"No, Thomas. Listen."

The shouts were wild and without words.

"Only the valley folks. People we know. See, there's Tad Walker." A rock crashed through the window onto the bed. Moonlight lay shattered on the starmeadow quilt. Thomas shook off the splintered glass as he jumped to the floor. He pulled up his overall straps as he ran to the door.

"Tad Walker!" he yelled.

"We want the egg!" Stenhouse shouted. The flaming thorn tree flickered red against their skull-white faces.

"The egg!" Miss Perryable screamed.

For an instant Thomas laughed inwardly at sight of this neglected woman whose hair in the shifting light coiled and uncoiled about her neck and crept like the black shadows of secret thoughts across her forehead. "The egg!" she screamed and the other women chorused the cry.

Thomas's scalp flinched. His spine arched as though he had been stuck with a spear in the small of his back. The shiver ended. He stood ready with clenched fists.

"We don't want to hurt you!"

"Then by God don't try to take the egg."

"Don't talk to the heathen!" Miss Perryable ran to the steps. The mob surged after her. Thomas planted his feet on each side the door. The sill cut into the corns on his soles. He braced himself.

A rock clipped through the air and gashed his temple. Thomas dived into the mob at the foot of the steps. For a moment a groaning beast with sixty legs and arms struggled and expanded and convulsed and opened up and gave birth to a dead man. For a second they stood back separately in regard, then dashed up the steps.

Miranda stood barefoot in the middle of the room. She bent forward and hugged the egg to her breast. She butted at the mob with the top of her head. Frightened hands shoved her from side to side and spun her about. "Thomas!" she screamed. They moved in close. Straightening herself and standing with fear white in her face and white on her closed eyelids, she whispered, "Papa. Papa."

In a charmed circle the crowd stood round her. There was an instant of lull. Then Stenhouse reached out toward her with a dry hand. At the touch of his blunt fingertips, the egg cracked open, empty, hollow. The two halves fell to the floor and filled like pools with shadows. The crowd stood awed, staring at the hollow shells which seemed to them like two deep sad eyes staring back in wonder from the cabin floor. Their voices rose and fell with it and faded to a hush.

Dumbly they pushed out of the cabin. Only Tad Walker

had courage to speak. "We're decent folks!" he hollered at the dark gaping door. He seized the burning thorn tree and slung it to the porch roof. Blindly they stumbled down the hillside, through the dusty bushes, to the bottomland road, where breathing in gulps they stared away from each other, and from old Huldah who sat in the ditch waiting, and parted without speaking.

Ordinarily after a marvel like an eclipse or a visit from an outsider or after a natural disaster like a hailstorm or an ax-fight, the valley folks like to stand around and tell each other how it happened and always the stories vary in every essential way, but the sum total of them is the truth which for a while escapes them.

This night they did not care to talk. Without looking into each other's blanched faces and hollow eyes, or back at the cabin which was blazing on the hillside, they made their separate ways to their separate houses, there to sit in the dark windows listening with fear to what they imagined to be the rustling of wings overhead but which in reality was only the familiar scattering of a west wind in the dry trees. Thus they sat in the long winter night, waiting for rain.

When the valley folks speak now of drought, they are liable to stare toward the Marrow place at the black chimney which they call Miranda's Tomb; and when they go over the mountain to Troy Town for a new plowshare, they always look deep into a certain spot in the Hickory Styx river where they say the silly speckled chickens marched that night and drowned themselves.

FROM THE
FRENCH QUARTER

We are sitting on a gallery in the French Quarter of New Orleans. Through the lacy iron grille of the balustrade we can see the cathedral, the steeple lighted and lost from moment to moment in the cumulus scud blowing in from the river beyond the coffeehouses. Tonight, a Friday night, our voices are, from moment to moment, lost in the jazz noise from Bourbon Street.

We are sitting, Jack Robillard and I, on the balcony where during the fall before we sat many late afternoons during my bachelor days. Now, on her first visit South, Kathy, my New England wife, is overcome by the oppressive June heat and is stretched out, fully clothed, with an electric fan ruffling first her fair hair, then her white dress, then her hair again. The fan is close enough to the couch to blow mosquitoes away. The tall windows in the living room where she is lying are open wide; and I can see by the

quick way she flicks pages of a fashion magazine that she
is too annoyed by the heat, mosquitoes, and by blisters on
her heels from the day's walking to sleep. I suggest she is
annoyed that Robillard is staying so late, drinking so much
gin, and, more directly, using so much ice which before
morning she may need to roll into a cloth and hold to her
wrists and forehead while waiting for another dawn which
will be white with heat.

Robillard is talking, his voice soft as the delta mud, but
crusted over with Eastern-prep-school pronunciations, in-
tonations. Robby was a football player at Tulane when I
was here before. His mother owns the house where I lived
then, where we are staying now as her guests; and I had
met him first when he came by, on behalf of his mother, to
pick up a rent check which I had forgotten to mail.

Although he had been, the previous fall, a star fullback,
he was not, I believe, an ambitious player for he never,
even during training, refused a drink. He had, in fact, got
in the habit of stopping by once or twice a week to sit and
drink and talk. The house and the magnificent Directoire
furnishings had belonged to his great-grandfather who lived
in it nine months a year and closed it during the summer
when he took his family back to France. Robby knew every
piece of furniture in my apartment and for a long time I
suspected he was coming by to be certain I was not ruin-
ing it.

This hot summer evening he is staring at a mahogany
box on the cast-iron garden table between us. The box is
about twice the size of a cigar box and may at one time
have been outfitted as a field desk. Its top has a polish so
high it catches, holds, reflects the steady glow of the citro-
nella candles. In the center of the top, a silver square has
been inlaid, but the engraved initials have been worn almost smooth; the edges are inlaid with silver and altogether it is a handsome thing. My wife and I have paid too

much for it and have done penance this evening by eating an omelet and salad at home rather than a salmon at Brennan's.

Robillard, as do most people who are accustomed to intense heat, moves only when necessary and then only with a minimum of effort. He raises his eyes, which even in the light from the candelabra are coldly blue, and asks, almost apologetically: "Where did you find it?"

For a moment I think he may be believing I have found the box in his attic or in what was once the wine cave. Even four thousand miles and two hundred years away from France, there is about some of these Creole families a little of the Parisian *méfiance*. I tilt the box open to show him the gold label and price tag of an antique shop on Royal Street.

He is far too polite to read the label or the price. He glances into his drink, then sips it slowly. "Here in New Orleans?" I nod. "Here in the Quarter?" I nod again: "On Royal Street."

"Boxes like that are—" he hesitates "—expensive, aren't they?" His wide brow flushes to the roots of his Norman blond hair, and the muscles in his huge jaw move as if he were chewing the words. Any mention of money pains him: once he borrowed two dollars from me and paid it back, without mentioning it, by leaving it in an envelope on the table in the reception hall. It is, perhaps, because of this almost ridiculous politeness that the other football players had called him, in mockery, "The Monster."

"It's a fine box." He touches the silver keyhole, tentatively. "Does it lock?"

I open the box again and show him the key Scotch-taped to the purple leather lining.

"That's a *good* box," he says. "It's a very old one, you know. An escritoire."

I ask how he knows.

"My grandfather had one somewhat like it," he says. The "somewhat" is emphasized to relieve me from my worry that I am under suspicion of having stolen the one his grandfather owned. His tactfulness often borders on insult and I sometimes have thought that his manners hide a basic arrogance and even contempt. For that reason I sometimes answer what I think he is saying rather than what he says.

"But his didn't have the silver?" I touch the inlay. I enjoy chiding him.

"Gold, as a matter of fact." He is lying and knows I know he is lying yet refuses to smile enough to make a pleasantry of it. It is one of the subtle ways he lets you know you are not from his world.

"Was that," I ask with a hint of taunt, "the grandfather who was King of Rex?"

He himself despises the entire debutante season of Mardi Gras and only because he is compelled by his mother does he attend the functions; but he will not make fun of it with a damn New Yorker. The term "damn New Yorker" he let slip in reference to me one evening when he was drinking more than usual. He had been angry because he could not stop the other football players from calling him The Monster. "Boomboy," a tackle who nicknamed him Monster, was that evening the target for his scorn: "I wish I were a damned New Yorker like him, and you."

"King of Rex?" he asks. His eyebrow arches. "No, I don't remember telling you that. My grandmother was Queen of Comus." His tone indicates even I should realize that the difference between Rex and Comus is perhaps the difference between silver and gold. He continues to study the box without touching it.

A mosquito bites my knuckle and immediately a hard white knob appears on it when I double my fist. The mosquitoes seem not to bite him ever and he looks away from my concern with the knuckle as though it is bad form to admit that mosquitoes exist.

"What are you going to do with it?" he asks.

"It'll go away." I regard the mosquito bite.

"With the box?" he says. His eyes indicate he has been drinking too much and there is a threat of violence in his voice and face. I have heard at Tulane that he can be a mean drunk and I dare not chide him more.

During the winter he has written that the students no longer consider him the perfect gentleman and therefore are no longer calling him The Monster. Since being back in town I have discovered why. One evening, drunk, he slapped a girl in a sorority house, jumped off the porch, ran through a boxwood hedge; and word had, as he knew it would, got round that he was not the embodiment of social graces, the debutantes' delight, the dream of all mothers. Then he had, or so rumor claimed, kneed an Ole Miss cheerleader in the groin while two of his teammates held the lad against the Bourbon House wall. It was perhaps after that the nickname was dropped, even among the athletes who had made most fun of his gentlemanly ways. It is an ugly story and I choose to disbelieve it.

"I don't know," I say vaguely, for I have forgotten the question while seeing in my mind the cheerleader slumping on the sidewalk and the three college boys running through the alleys of the Quarter.

"Then why did you buy it?" he asks, and then he says something which I cannot quite hear.

"I liked it."

He looks up suddenly and as though I can be surprised into action says: "Give it to me."

"Why should I give it to you?"

"It's a good box."

"I know it is. That's why we bought it."

"But I need it."

"Why do you need it?"

He smiles, rather drunkenly, without answering.

"What do you need it for?"

He shakes his head.

"Maybe if I know what you want it for, we can think about it." Through the tall windows I can see that Kathy has let the magazine slip to the Turkey rug, her fingertips still touching it. She breathes deeply, asleep, exhausted at last by the heat. The electric fan is droning as it does when overheated.

Robillard shakes his head; he is not ready to tell me. Finally he quits smiling and sips a little from his glass, barely wetting his full bottom lip.

"Then sell it to me."

"What for? Why?" All this is completely out of character for him: to mention another person's possessions other than in casual, passing admiration.

"It's a *good* box." He smiles as though he himself realizes what a good box it is and what a good joke it would be for him to possess it. He glances up, his eyes as alight with merriment as those of a child who has seen an unexpected frog.

"What happened to the box that belonged to your grandfather?" I asked.

He pauses for a long time and gazes at the cathedral steeple which the scud is revealing. His voice when he answers has that monotone which people usually reserve for the relating of dreams. "Do you realize that I never got to answer a telephone unless my mother talked first with the person and knew who it was? I never went to a movie, even in daytime, unless she knew exactly where it was, what it was, and the name of every person I would be with. If I went out at night she knew everything about every family of every girl and boy I'd be with. I didn't even open my own letters. They were open and arranged on my desk

when I got home from school. There was no way to have a
secret from my mother."

I do not see that he is answering the question about the
box that belonged to his grandfather, but he continues:
"There wasn't a lock in the house with a key, not to my
room, not even to the bathroom. Even my desk couldn't
be locked. There wasn't one key in the house until I was
eleven years old."

"You bought one."

"My grandfather died and my grandmother gave me this
box like that one."

"And it had a key?"

"It had a good key and I took the key everywhere with
me, even to sleep. My mother never got to touch it and fur-
thermore," he says with determination, "she'd better never
try."

His eleven-year-old pride is in his voice, and a new,
amused tone. "I kept all my treasures in the box and she
never saw in it."

"What sort of treasures?" I ask.

His face becomes crafty, then mocking, and he laughs a
little drunkenly: "Aha! You want to know too. Then you
and my mother will get together and she'll wheedle the se-
crets out of you."

I join his game, cross my heart, raise my right hand, and
hope to die rather than reveal the contents of the box, the
nature of his treasures.

But he shakes his head. "Before I went off to school, I
took all my treasures out and buried them in a Maxwell
House coffee can under the arbor." He looks cagey again.
"You think I'm talking about the arbor in the camellia garden, but you're wrong!"

"And you left the box empty and went off to school?"

"Certainly not. I took it with me. And the key."

"To Andover?"

"To Phillips, yes," he nods, "and to Princeton."

"Where is it now?" I ask.

"I still have it." He shows me the key on the heavy watch chain which, along with an elegant watch in a hunter's case, had come to him from his grandfather.

"But then," I say, "if you still have a box, you don't need ours."

"But mine is full," he says, toying with the brass key which is tangled in the chain. "Yours is empty. Mine won't hold even a bank check more. But with that one I could start all over again."

I actually do not expect an answer but I take a chance and whisper in melodramatic suspense: "What is in your box?"

He untangles the key and then stares at me with a level, sober look. "Letters from my mother," he says coldly.

We talked only a little more about the box on the table between us, and I refused to sell it to him that evening. But later, when my wife and I were back in New York and received an announcement that he was marrying a girl from New Orleans, and that they would be At Home in the Garden District, we sent him the box as a wedding present. The note from his bride was correct and concise, and the handwriting clear and firm.

PROMISCUOUS
UNBOUND

"Wonder what their children will be like?" Mrs. Molly Bloom had no more than dragged her lace veil through the church door before Mrs. Oliver (of the Fat Olivers) bull-dozed through the crowd and asked, "Wonder what their children will be like?"

"Like rabbits, probably." Mrs. Harry did not try to hide her feelings about her new son-in-law. "If I know Mr. W. R. Goatt."

Perhaps a more prophetic statement was never shouted in the South Side Baptist Church. During the next five years Molly Bloom and Mr. Goatt had five children: Matthew, Mark, Luke, John—and Little Acts who became known as "Mutt" because Matthew was the first word he tried to say and "Mutt" was what it sounded like.

They tell the story about Mutt two ways in our town. Some say he was a most unusual baby, raising their eyebrows all over the place, but then people are apt to remember more than ever happened when a tragedy finally occurs. They even quote Nurse Emmie Davis, who everybody knows is so nearsighted she hasn't even seen her own mirror in years, that Mutt as a baby was a *sight*. Well, you can't tell this long afterward. Maybe he was. But then there are the other people, friends largely of the family, who say he was like any baby and child in the world until he met Mrs. Ludie Shaggs.

Mrs. Shaggs, to tell the truth, was a striking blonde creature—double-breasted if ever a woman was. She carried herself like a pouter pigeon and all the children in the neighborhood bet that she had to sleep on her back to keep from feeling like she was sleeping uphill. They had visions of her, lying there prone, like a board on a seesaw, with sometimes her head stuck into the air and at other times her feet. Probably neither did, but that's what all the children reckoned. No one knew much about Mr. Shaggs except that he carried an umbrella and raised dahlias as big as derby hats and was liable to keep any football that landed in his flower-bed.

Anyway, it was there one afternoon that B. B. Nelson punted a ball over his back fence into the Shaggs garden. Although Mr. Shaggs had never been known to speak to a child in the neighborhood, it was understood that any boy caught alive in that back yard wouldn't live to remember it. Both teams went over to the wooden fence and peeped through the cracks at the football where it lay side by side with a purple dahlia almost as large. Even children could see that the flower was a prize-winner. They didn't say as much. They merely said, "Uh oh," and Sissy Burton remembered that his mother wanted him that minute. If Sissy hadn't run out the driveway they probably would have thrown him over the fence and dared him to come back without the ball. As it was they stood back, stared angrily at each other, and then at B.B. who had punted the ball. B.B. searched the ground and then the back steps where little Mutt Goatt sat, mouth open, whittling with a butcher knife.

Mutt was only five, not quite six, at the time and didn't know anything about the Shaggses. Or maybe he did know and just didn't care. You couldn't tell about Mutt. They watched him whittling and decided he was the one to send. Mr. Shaggs might have mercy on such a little boy.

A rope was tied around Mutt's waist, and B.B. and his brother, sitting on the fence rail, lowered Mutt into the Shaggses' garden. He crouched down behind a peony bush, just as he had been coached to do, and tried to untie the rope. Finally, when he couldn't, the boys whispered through the fence: "Go on. Get the ball. We'll meet you out front."

The boys ran halfway round the block and stood in front of the Shaggses' house to wait for Mutt to come running, rope trailing, out the drive, with the football that cost, they remembered now, eighty-nine cents, almost a dollar. Five minutes passed and they were still waiting.

Thirty minutes later seven of the boys were sitting on the stone wall in front of the Shaggses', looking up the lawn at the old house. On the other side four of the boys were seated on the wooden fence staring moodily down into the garden where little Mutt had last been seen. The football was gone; but so was the beheaded dahlia.

Ten more minutes passed and the boys on the back fence began seeing signs of what must have been a struggle in the garden. At about the same time it came to all the boys on the front wall that Mr. Shaggs had bound Mutt and tossed him in the coal hopper. They joined forces at the corner, marched up the street, and bravely up the drive to the basement window. B.B. Nelson was ready to punt the glass in when they heard the clink of a spoon above. There tapping on the pane with an ice cream spoon was Mutt. Before him was a water goblet half full of lime sherbet and behind him in full bloom was Mrs. Shaggs.

Late that afternoon, long after he had tossed the football from the Shaggses' porch to the waiting boys, Mutt came sauntering up the street, carrying the purple dahlia on the upraised palms of his hands.

He kept the flower before his plate during supper, and his breathing which was always heavy was a rumbling sigh tonight.

"Don t breathe like that!" Mrs. Molly Bloom said.

"Can't help it," Mutt said, still gazing at the gaudy purple flower which he was touching lightly with his fingertips.

"We're going to have to have his adenoids taken out," Mr. W.R. said.

"My what!" Mutt glanced up in alarm.

"Adenoids." Mr. W.R. explained what and where and why about the adenoids.

"Oh," Mutt said.

He took the flower to bed with him that night and used it as a pillow. He lay on his back, hands joined under his head, the flower under his hands. About two o'clock an autumn storm churned through town and Mrs. Molly went in to see if Mutt was covered up. He was still lying there, eyes wide, staring at the ceiling.

"Did the storm wake you?" she asked.

"What storm?" he said.

After that it was a fresh flower every day—huge dahlias: purple, dark red, white, and yellow, but mostly purple. Mutt tried to press them between the pages of his Gulliver book but the flowers were too large and fat for that, so he kept them in a wheelbarrow under the house. He could not be persuaded to throw dead flowers away and he could not be kept from running off to the Shaggses'.

"Does Mr. Shaggs know you're picking his prettiest flowers?" Mrs. Molly asked. "Who gives them to you?"

"Ludie," Mutt said casually. He smiled at the flower in hand.

"Who is Ludie?"

"Her," Mutt said. "Mrs. Shaggs."

"Ludie! We'll have a little more respect out of you, young man. Now don't let me hear you say 'Ludie' again."

Mutt laughed at the flower, tossed it into the air, and caught it. He was out the door and down the street to the Shaggses' before Mrs. Molly could warn him again.

It was two days later that he came home smelling of smoke. He had already been to the pantry and eaten peanut butter, but he still smelled of tobacco and smoke.

"Have you been smoking?" W.R. asked at supper.

"No," Mutt said.

Mrs. Molly, sitting next to him, sniffed at the top of his head and at his ears.

"You most certainly have," she said, "or else you've been mighty close to somebody who has."

"Lu—" Mutt began. "Mrs. Shaggs kissed me goodbye."

"Oh," Mrs. Molly sighed with relief.

W.R. chuckled.

"Does Mr. Shaggs know you kiss his wife goodbye?"

"Oh hell no!" Mutt said, red as the flower before his plate.

"Probably just as well," W.R. said.

It wasn't until the next morning that Mrs. Molly realized Mutt had said a cuss word, and whipped him for it. He was furious. He stalked out of the house and did not return until dark. He had eaten, he said, both lunch and dinner (not dinner and supper, mind you) at the Shaggses'. He wouldn't eat anything even before he went to bed, but at three o'clock that morning they found him in the kitchen drinking black coffee. He didn't look very happy.

Mrs. Molly and her husband stood there in the door and watched him.

"Are you sick?" Molly asked.

"No." Mutt rubbed his chin as though to see if he needed a shave. "Just couldn't sleep."

"W.R., something's got to be done," she said.

"For instance?" her husband asked.

"Well, for one thing, he's got to stay away from that Shaggs woman."

"Promise your mother you'll stay away from Ludie Shaggs," his father said.

"I won't."

"You won't what?"

"I won't promise."

"Can't say as I blame you." Mr. Goatt winked, clicked his tongue, and went back to bed.

"What either of you sees in that blonde hussy!" Mrs. Molly was saying as she followed my uncle down the dark hall. "Poor fools."

The iron grille gate at the end of the walk was shut and locked the next morning and Mutt was promised a whipping if he went out of the yard or even so much as touched the gate or the iron-spike pickets of the front fence. He was allowed to play on the wooden fence enclosing the back yard but warned that if he had any ideas about falling, he'd better commence planning immediately to fall in his own yard, and preferably on his feet.

That week he played in the yard, Mrs. Molly occasionally watching from various windows and his brothers reporting during the day that he was still in the yard, had not been seen out of it. Yet each night he came in with a gleam and a flower. Apparently he was happy: he ate well, he slept well, he laughed, and he was learning to whistle. As the autumn days grew shorter, colder, more full of falling leaves, Mutt became more restless. He wandered about the front yard, cheeks puffed out, lips puckered, whistling the strangest whistle you ever heard, more like the piping of a broken kettle than anything, at times scarcely hearable, at times shrill. When a woman would pass down the street, Mutt would head for the gate and, with fingers between teeth, whistle. It was disconcerting.

So disturbing in fact that Preacher Clement stopped to ask if the young man in the yard would not be more happily occupied if allowed to play with other children his own age. Of course Mrs. Molly could not explain to the preacher why Mutt was being kept in; or at least she thought she couldn't, not knowing it was a public secret.

"Then at least," Preacher Clement pleaded, "can he be prevailed upon to refrain from this whistling after women. My wife has become so haunted by it she's taken to going to town by Mulberry Street, two whole blocks out of the way." Then he added painfully, "Through my instructions." He mumbled, Mrs. Molly still believes, something to the effect that his wife was all he had and that he wasn't the only husband who was worried about the recent behavior of several of the ladies who had to pass this way. Whatever he meant, Mrs. Molly was touched by his tone and manner. So much so that she decided to let Mutt out. But when later in the afternoon she saw Mrs. Ludie Shaggs talking to him at the front fence and even reaching through to pat him on the head (right there in open daylight, before God and all the neighbors, if you can imagine) she was so upset she almost changed her mind.

It wouldn't have made any difference what she decided because the next morning Mutt did not come down to breakfast. He was not in his bed, his room, the house, or yard.

About four o'clock Mr. Shaggs phoned and said with no

more ceremony than a banker: "Where's my wife?"

Mrs. Molly declared she didn't know.

"She damn well better be home before dark!" He slammed down the receiver before she could ask him if he'd seen Mutt.

At dark, Mr. Goatt answered the telephone.

"Where's my wife?" the angry voice said.

"Where's my son?" Mr. Goatt said, equally as angry because he had heard of the earlier call.

"I don't know. But I do know where he'll be if he sets foot in my house again. Or if another of my dahlias is missing!" He slammed down the receiver.

"I think that man is unhappy," Mr. Goatt said.

"You think he meant that threat?"

"Certainly. I tell you he's unhappy."

"The frost will probably take care of the flowers soon anyhow," Mrs. Molly said hopefully.

"Frost won't take care of Mutt though. It's time he's taught to be discreet, if nothing else." Fortunately he was asleep when Mutt crept in after midnight.

No one knows yet how Mr. Goatt intended teaching his son to be discreet, but the beginning did seem to be inspired simplicity. Some people say Mr. Goatt picked up the idea while he was training horses in the horse cavalry, but it doesn't make much difference now. What he did was this: he stretched a wire, strong as a cable, tight as possible, from the corner of the house to a tree near the wood fence. On this he hitched a chain leash, and to the leash a collar, and in the collar Mutt. He locked it with a little lock and took the key with him because Mrs. Molly was already crying at the sight of her son on a leash. Every time little Mutt ran, the chain rattled and Mrs. Molly had to cover her ears or dry her eyes. Finally she put cotton in her ears and stayed on the other side of the house.

Just before dinner, however (she had worked her way

to the upstairs, where she had begun making the beds), it occurred to her, she doesn't know why, to look out of the window. Sure enough, two back yards away, in the dahlia garden, Mrs. Shaggs in a red and white flowered kimono, was cutting a huge blossom. She held it first in her hair and from the upstairs window it looked like a flop-hat. She must have known how foolish it appeared because then she held it to her low neckline, between her mighty bosoms. She must have been delighted with the effect because she pinned it there, then tossed her blonde hair back over her shoulder in one quick lift of her chin.

Ten minutes later when Mrs. Molly stuck her head out of the window to tell Mutt to come to the back steps for his dinner, he was gone. Mrs. Shaggs was gone too. The broken leash was hanging empty from the wire.

Mrs. Molly went straightway to the phone and called her husband: "W.R., she's got him. Came right into the yard and took him."

"That kid!" W.R. said proudly.

"What?" Mrs. Molly Bloom was shouting.

"Real sex appeal."

"Mrs. Shaggs?"

"The kid."

"Oh." Mrs. Molly sounded relieved. Then: "What are we going to do?"

"Just wait. He'll come back when he gets tired."

They waited all night and until noon the next day. At lunch W.R. said: "Maybe he's not going to get tired."

"Quit leering and finish your coffee." Mrs. Molly was already taking dishes from the table.

It was then that the phone rang. Mr. Shaggs was dead. The children were already chanting the news in the street. "Dead in the bed with a bullet in his head."

All afternoon a crowd fringed the Shaggs house, peeping

in at the shade-drawn windows, searching the garage, and rambling curiously in the flower garden. His car, everyone knew, was gone; his wife and her clothes, some said, were gone; and even though Mrs. Molly tried to keep it a secret, someone, then everyone, knew that Mutt was gone. The death was explained in the only four possible ways: Mr. Shaggs had killed himself upon discovering his wife's elopement; Mrs. Shaggs had killed him to escape; Mutt had accidentally killed him; Mutt had killed him intentionally.

To complicate matters, Sissy Burton then began feeling guilty that he had not allowed himself to be thrown over the fence that autumn day to get the football. He confessed in the front yard that he had done the killing. Everyone thought he was bragging and so ignored him. Then he got to feeling so guilty he was afraid they would believe him and went around declaring that he had not done the killing.

Somehow it was very casual. "After all," Preacher Clement said, "you can't take the actions of a six-year-old boy seriously." He glanced about the crowd, nervously searching for his wife in the gathering dusk. "I do hope," she was saying with a sparkling gleam in her eye, "that they find that boy before Ludie Shaggs goes very far with him."

"If you ask me," W.R. began, "she's already . . ."

"Nobody did. So shut up." Mrs. Molly could not keep him from praising Mutt's accomplishments and persistence. That night they left the door open and the coffeepot on in case Mutt should sneak back. It was a restless night for the entire neighborhood. Lights in every house flashed on, burned brightly for a while, then as suddenly went off.

Toward dawn, which was cold and gray, Ludie Shaggs drove up to her house, blew her horn to wake the two policemen who were keeping watch in the patrol car, and then went with them down to the jail. She claimed she did not know her husband was dead when she left town with

Mutt. She had packed her clothes that afternoon, left Mutt in the house bathing while she went down to have the car checked. It was during that half-hour that her husband must have come home and found Mutt in the tub. According to Mrs. Shaggs, Mutt said there had been an argument through the locked bathroom door in which Mr. Shaggs threatened to kill him if he ever came in the house again. Mutt, looking for a towel, found the pitsol in the bathroom linen closet, opened the door, and walked into the bedroom.

"Let me have that, sonny," Mr. Shaggs said, sitting down on the bed. Mutt, in his simple way, walked up to him and let him have it, right in the head.

"He was as calm as I'd ever seen him," Mrs. Shaggs was sobbing when W.R. appeared at the police station. "Was waiting for me on the back steps. Had dragged my suitcase out into the yard. 'The house is all locked,' he told me. I tried the back door and it was locked. I didn't know Mr. Shaggs had already come home. We left in a hurry because it was almost time for him."

"Where did you last see the boy?" Mr. W.R. asked.

"At a tavern on the other side of Atlanta, Georgia. Drinking beer with two college girls in a convertible. I'd gone to see about a cabin and when I got back there he was with these two bi—biddies." She sobbed. "I said, 'Come on, Mutt, we got a cabin.' He said, 'Pipe down, Grandma.' I went to the cabin and watched him from the window. The way he was carrying on with those two girls! Right there before my eyes. And them squealing and acting so damned coy. They had the radio going and that's how he knew the police were already after us. He came in and told me what I've done told you. I said, "Let's get out of here. Florida maybe.' I was scared. 'Beat it,' he said, 'I'm sticking with them.' He jerked his thumb over his shoulder at the convertible outside. I could tell by watching him as

he got back in the car that he was already far gone with
one of the girls—the blonde. I started out after him. I
chased them a good fifteen miles before they lost me."

The more they checked the more the police believed
Mrs. Shaggs's story. The fingerprints on the gun were
Mutt's, and Hank Beatty, the garage man, testified that
Mrs. Shaggs was with him during that half-hour in which
neighbors remembered hearing the shot. When he married
Ludie a year later half the town wanted to reopen the case,
but the other half wanted fervently to forget the whole
affair, and more specially to forget Mutt.

As happens with the memory of most ruggedly defined
and active men, a cloud of rumor sprang up around the
memory of Mutt to soften the ruggedness and hide the
spectacular differences. He was never heard from directly
again. A tabloid claimed he was smuggled across the Mexi-
can border in a baby carriage by a silent-movie vampire.
Other people said she took him to Hollywood where he
wouldn't be noticed. Some claimed it was to New York
where he would be appreciated. Others claimed he was
forced by a Chicago gangster to take a vow of silence and
withdraw from society.

Just before the war a psychologist settled in the town
and put forward the theory that Mutt never really existed,
that he was merely the six-year-old in all of us, that he was
the town's knowing myth. A good many people began believing the psychologist but when he went off to the war,
Preacher Clement, who had objected violently to the theory, put forward the notion that perhaps the psychologist
had never really existed—an idea that many people found
just as attractive. Anyway, Mrs. Ludie Shaggs had courage
enough to come back and live, knowing that people were
pointing her out and talking about her, as they did and do,
even to this very day.

THE YEAR OF
THE LILY-BLIGHT

Few people in the town, in fact no one except Mr. Jesse Hugh, who is actively engaged in the growing of lilies, have even considered, except momentarily at Easter time, and then only because of the increase in price, that there is a blight killing off the lilies.

Other things are happening in Weal, North Carolina (pop. 27,600), which are commanding the attention of the townsfolk.

The Weal Commonwealth (circulation 12,000) reported the second day of January that a dead baby had been found in a Tumble-Dry unit at the Wash Palace. For three days there were various speculations during coffee breaks. In the Thrall Building, the only skyscraper in the city, the consensus at the soda fountain was that a mother and father had arrived home from a New Year's celebration and had accidentally gathered up the baby with the blankets.

173

Since there was evidence that the blankets had not been washed, this theory was gradually abandoned.

When the identity of the year-old baby was finally learned, the fact seemed less likely than the speculation. A divorcée, visiting her husband's relatives during the holidays, and staying in Bide Time Tourist Court, had, almost asleep, instructed her five-year-old daughter to take the crying baby out and if he were wet to dry him. When it was proved by the coroner that the five-year-old girl could not, even by standing on one of the metal chairs in the Wash Palace, reach the coin slot to deposit a dime in the Tumble-Dry unit, the newspaper printed the fact under the headline "FOUL PLAY AT WORK." However, after being questioned regularly by trained personnel, the little girl persisted in her statement which was accepted as a conclusion: "A tall man put the money in for me." Who the tall stranger was, no one could discover. After a time, interest in the identity of the stranger was lost.

Soon after ground hog day, "Daddy" Dan Fricks, who in any other town would have been known by his beard, dark glasses, and like by his vocabulary, man, as a "beatnik," got hung up on the word "yonder." For close on to two weeks in February he repeated the word aloud, to himself or to anyone who cared to listen, a few friends at first, but later a sizable crowd for a bar the size of Marino's, sixteen thousand times a day without stopping. Buddy Groves who in summer acted as lifeguard at Beetle Beach counted with the automatic counter which he had stolen from the gate boy.

Sarah Osgrove who was twenty-five and the last unmarried girl in her crowd was out the first morning of March at dawn. She sat in the porch swing and announced to her mother that she was just going to sit there until something happened in that town. Even though she went out punctually every morning at seven and sat there all day except at mealtime, nothing happened during the entire month of March. So April first she announced that she had every intention of doing the same thing the month of April. And she did. May and June too.

"Nobody tells me what to eat," said Nick Antonio. And he sat down on the Fourth of July and ate an entire barbecued pig. Much to no one's surprise, Nick Antonio was dead by midnight from a cerebral hemorrhage, though no one could profess to see anything cerebral about his concourse with the pig. Only one person even remarked that he had failed to swallow the smile from the pig's face, for there in truth it was, stretched tight on the face of the corpse. It made one wonder who had eaten whom.

Of passing interest at the Weal Charity Hospital during the August dog days was the case of Muriel Robinson, aged eighteen, who had become so terrified of her shadow that she had to be blindfolded while being transported from one dark room to another. The shadow, she claimed, was not her own.

"I feel faint," said Mrs. Nannie Snow in the back seat of the automobile driven by her grandson.

"Miss Nannie," as she was called, was ninety-four that September and subject to car sickness. But she still insisted each Sunday on being driven through Weal and down the White Horse Road.

"Shall I stop, Miss Nannie?" her grandson called back.

"Just as you please," she more or less croaked. "I just feel faint."

When the car was finally eased onto the grassy shoulder, Oscar Snow jumped out from behind the wheel and helped the old lady out.

She stood, steadied herself on the door, then toddled forward across the field. After five or six steps she turned in baby-fashion and looked back, as though for applause. Reassuring herself that she had their full attention, she stumbled on, only occasionally using her cane.

It being a warm day for September, her grandson and his wife strolled along at a respectful distance behind her.

At a small cedar tree in the center of the field she stopped.

When the younger couple reached her she was saying to the tree: "Young man, I asked you: Whose field is this and if you can't tell me that maybe you can tell me did it by any chance once belong to a family name of Locum or Locust or something like that. No. Benjamin Locum. That's the name."

After that, the Snows referred to that Sunday as the day Miss Nannie talked to a Tree. But not within her hearing.

Perhaps in not unrelated fashion, at the Weal City Park Zoo, at the beginning of October, there were, by Zoo records, six captive vultures. The month was almost over before Kenny Keith, an Attendant (for such was the word on the buzzard-keeper's cap), reported that there were only five birds, with, he also reported, "knowing sort of looks." He was not fired and he was not asked to resign his post; but, as he said, he knew which way the wind was blowing, and it was agreed that with his experience he certainly should know. Later he appeared with the same regularity at his new work as a janitor at the jail where, by coincidence, at the beginning of that month, there were five inmates.

Along the ridge of Bellow Mountain, beginning that fall, two men patrolled the old Peau Rouge trail, one from north south, the other from south north, one from eight to two, the other from two to eight and each with a Geiger counter. When asked "Wherefore?" by hunters, boy scouts, lovers, and hog-herders, they answered: "Prospecting."

The truth was they were Security men from an unpublicized atomic plant on the other side of the mountain. Usually, at least at this early, red stage of the autumn, the dry chirp of the crickets was louder than the metallic click of their gadgets.

The Sunday after Thanksgiving, Dr. Elmo Fier, vegetarian, segregationist, white, married, Protestant, suburban, owner of a station wagon, a barbecue grill, four Van Gogh reproductions, a kidney-shaped coffee table, two form-fitting plastic chairs—in short, a progressive man, with graying temples, balding pate, varicose veins, a paunch, and pains indicative of duodenal ulcers—ended a stirring speech to a joint meeting of the Young Business Men's Club and the Auxiliary Lady Voters with the admonishment to consider the lilies of the field, how they toiled not and wanted not. Since it was neither a speech nor a sermon, no one knew exactly what to do, but the majority applauded not.

But, as has been said, only Mr. Jesse Hugh who was actively engaged in the growing of lilies was aware of the lily-blight and from Thanksgiving on he began spending as much time on his knees in his bedroom, praying, as in the same position in his greenhouse, pruning.

As for the rest of the town: the clerks and typists in the Thrall Building (sixteen stories) are talking during their coffee breaks of the newest murders; Muriel Robinson is confined to a permanently dark room where there is no likelihood of her seeing her shadow; "Daddy" Fricks continues, with the aid now of marijuana and more, to be seized by spells of "yonder"; Sara Osgrove, still unmarried, sits on the porch swing waiting for something to happen; the widow of Nick Antonio puts flowers on his grave every Sunday and during the week refuses pork; Miss Nannie Snow has found a tree in her own yard to which she talks secretly about a secret past; Kenny Keith, the buzzard-keeper, is unduly alarmed when he counts by mistake four instead of five men in his charge; and on the ridge of Bellow Mountain, the two Security men walk with their Geiger counters clicking—more audibly now that the crickets are silent.

WHAT TO DO TILL THE POSTMAN COMES

The two old men met early each afternoon on the pleasant wide porch and waited for the postman. The porch faced the park, the water, and the afternoon sun. There were glass jalousie windows which could be rolled shut when the winter wind came up across the Tampa Bay.

The two old men, Mr. Beattle, who had been a professor, and Mr. Kelley, a retired manufacturer, were as different in character as one could imagine; and yet this was the time of day they both waited for all morning. It was a time of easy comradeship, free from solitude, and safe from the inquisition of strangers who had no notion of privacy. There was, too, and more important, the possibility of mail.

"No, I haven't seen him yet." Mr. Beattle was seated in the light aluminum chair, his walking stick laid precisely across the arms, his feet in their highly polished black shoes and wool-rib socks placed side by side in a spot of sun that warmed the green sisal rug.

Mr. Kelley, breathing heavily, was coming up the three low steps. He pushed open the glass door. "I thought I heard him."

There was no need to comment on this and Mr. Beattle, who was from Virginia, remained silent in his tidewater way.

It was Mr. Beattle's impressive head that was a surprise each day to Mr. Kelley. Beattle had the sort of thick gray and sandy blond hair that stayed combed but nevertheless stood up and away from his head. With his shaggy eyebrows it gave him a leonine aspect and great dignity. He had practically no cheekbones so that there were slanting hollows from his deep-set eyes to his strong jaw. His teeth, too, in spite of their stains, still showed strong, and added to the vigorous feline countenance.

His body, though, was thin. In winter, when he wore his tweeds, he had the bearing of a large man; but now in the early fall with his sport shirt and narrow knit tie, he was plainly thin and old. Kelley often wondered if Mr. Beattle ate enough.

It was plain to anyone that Kelley had eaten enough all his life. His florid face sagged with weight; and folds of fat hung from his jawbones and swayed when he moved his head. His stomach was enormous and had the padded appearance his grandchildren liked to imitate with sofa cushions. His voice rolled in the deep, hearty manner of many fat men and made Mr. Beattle look smaller, as though he were shrinking to escape the voice which reverberated in the glass sunporch.

"Mr. Beattle," he said, "the sun's still hot."

Mr. Beattle nodded that that was true.

Mr. Kelley let the door close behind him and lowered his weight onto the green web of the aluminum chaise longue. His seersucker shirt was transparent where it stuck to his pink breasts and his green putter-trousers were as wrinkled as pajamas. He wore sandals and no socks. There were days, Beattle was sure, when Mr. Kelley tried to look as repulsive as possible.

On such days, Beattle had further noticed, Mr. Kelley was inclined to make personal remarks.

"Mr. Beattle," he said between breaths, "I don't see how you stand those wool trousers."

With his gray-haired fingers, the yellowed nails pared round and close, Beattle pinched the seams of his worsted flannels at the knees. He was inclined to say that he found them comfortable and was accustomed to them, but that would only open the way for more remarks from Mr. Kelley in his present mood.

When Mr. Beattle said nothing, Kelley watched him shrewdly out of the corner of his eye. He tried again: "Don't you sweat?"

Beattle was certain now that this was a bad day for Mr. Kelley. Even though the question was direct, he chose not to answer.

It was a bad time for Mr. Kelley. For three days he had had no mail. Yesterday he had walked straight from the porch to the Korner Store and had bought things that were not on his list: shrimp creole, poppyseed rolls, French Alsatian wine, a pint of ice cream, four different kinds of candy bars, and promising himself that he would portion these things out to himself over a two-week period, he'd gone home and eaten them all before midnight.

Twice he had awakened during the night with indigestion. This morning he felt not only fat but completely without character and had thought, as Beattle surmised: "To hell with socks. If I'm going to eat like one, I may as well look like one."

When Beattle had waited long enough for the porch to

echo with the brashness of the question about his sweat glands, he said, "It is warm today."

Kelley was disgusted with the cautious words. "Why does he have to weigh a damned statement like that? I'm not going to write it down and footnote it."

Beattle was thinking: "Lead him from the personal to the general."

"I sweat," Mr. Kelley said. "I imagine I sweat close to a half-gallon a day."

"That's sixty-four ounces," Mr. Beattle said, not really sure.

"Just about," Mr. Kelley said. "I won't miss it far." He could tell from the tightness about Mr. Beattle's mouth the exact degree to which he was annoying the man. He himself did not like to talk about perspiration and odors; and he respected and admired Mr. Beattle's sense of propriety. Yet, in his present mood, he felt it was good for Mr. Beattle to be offended a little every day. He made a great display now of wiping the creases of his neck and mopping the top of his brown, bald head and even the fringe of his white, curly hair. He stuffed his unironed handkerchief into the side pocket of his putter-pants.

Mr. Beattle, without glancing away from the bay, arranged his black knit tie so that it fell exactly down the center of his checked shirt.

"You haven't seen him yet?" Mr. Kelley remarked again about the postman.

"He'll probably be late today," Mr. Beattle said. "It still being close to the first of the month."

Neither of them spoke or glanced quickly at the other expecting conversation. They were settling now, by mutual, habitual agreement, into that period of silence that lasted sometimes twenty minutes, sometimes an hour, in which they looked out across the green park, at the old people sitting in the sun, or moving slowly with their canes or with their arms clasped to each other for support, along the curving walks, in and out of the sun under the feathery mimosas and the palm fronds which rattled in the constant breeze. Beyond were the yachts in the basin, their tall masts swaying slowly, and the younger men running up and down the wooden docks with buckets and sponges and hoses, calling to each other in the reserved way that people have about boats that are tied up, and calling to and giving orders to the few youngsters who, naked except for shorts and sneakers, jumped from dock to boatdeck, shouting in higher voices. And over them and over the bay which lay beyond the boat slips, the seagulls whirled and circled and dived, screeching in their shrill calls which imitated laughter.

From his desk at the double-window above the porch, Beattle could view the same scene and even the buoy markers with an indolent pelican on each. But when he was in his apartment he rarely looked down at the boulevard and the park and the sea. In the morning he would glance out at the sky but not to see the clearness of the blue or the shaping of the sea clouds, but to determine what sort of clothes to wear that day. Even during this quiet time with Mr. Kelley, he would watch the people only for a while and then he would read articles and extracts from his academic journals.

Kelley, who had a cottage in the back with a picture window that faced a graveled patio, a sterile banana tree, and a pink stucco wall, surveyed the scene from the porch with immense satisfaction, as though he had arranged it all and was quite pleased with the composition and especially with the line made by the red acacias which bordered the walks.

Sometimes Kelley counted the old people in the park and estimated how much they spent each month and figured in his head how much principal was necessary to yield that monthly income. It pleased him to know that he was surrounded by that many enterprising, conservative, prosperous people, many who, like himself, had started in business in really a very modest way and had been able to hand over to their children quite prospering concerns. His three sons, for instance, the youngest not yet fifty, could all three retire tomorrow if necessary.

Sometimes he counted the boats through one window only and figured the capital tied up at that one wooden dock. They represented to him a different sort of wealth and one of which he did not completely approve, even though twice, years ago, he himself had priced boats in showrooms and had escaped only by saying: "Let me phone you back in the morning." The boats would be bought by his sons or grandsons. He himself was too aware of money to spend it so freely. His slight feeling of disapproval was not enough to keep him from enjoying the sight of the full sails as a boat slid out into the bay, tipped, came about, and, gathering the full force of the breeze, skimmed toward the horizon.

Beattle stirred in his chair. The silence, having begun after a rather strained conversation, was not as comfortable as he ordinarily found it, and he wanted to show his equanimity by asking Mr. Kelley a question about the trading on yesterday's market which he was sure to find pleasure in explaining. But judging from Mr. Kelley's hands, curled and relaxed on his stomach, he decided that Mr. Kelley was absorbed in his own thoughts and not troubled by, if indeed he had noticed it, Beattle's early annoyance.

Beattle, too, looked back at the park and played his game. He liked to see it for a few minutes each day as a different painter would see it. He had begun the month before with the obvious choice of Cézanne. He had worked his way through the French Impressionists and then had searched backward through Watteau and the English and now was seeing it as Rembrandt might. He squinted his eyes till only the white sail shone brilliantly against the dark sea, and then opened them wide enough to catch lesser lights from a cloud, a water tank, and the top deck of another boat. He, too, had a feeling of gratification.

Being of a more contemplative mind than Kelley, he realized that the peaceful feeling came, not from the scene itself, but from the usually easy, uncompromising comradeship on the porch. Both of the men respected privacy and both of them had had in their winters here the disquieting experience of making acquaintances too hastily, from fear of loneliness, with people who not only did not revere privacy but who actually did not know that the need existed. As a result, both of them were sensitive to encroachments, their own and others.

Kelley, in one of his first winters here, had generously left his doors open so that his neighbors could come in without being invited, for a drink or to watch his TV which was one of the first sets in the city. One evening he had glanced about his living room-terrace and seen eleven people, three of whom he knew only by name, gazing at, fascinated by, a loud and senseless TV program. He had studied each of the dimly lighted, expressionless faces and asked: "Do I really like that person?" "Do I want to know him better?" Then he had asked the decisive question, feeling he had earned a right to a certain degree of selectivity: "Would I know that person back home?" The answer in nine of the cases was no. At that moment the two to whom he would have said yes, a frail little lady and her husband, an old lawyer from Vermont with snowy hair and brows, moved toward him, touched his hand and whispered, "Don't, don't," when Kelley started to rise. The lawyer had waved toward the TV set: "I don't understand all this." At the beginning of the gravel drive he clasped Kelley's hand.

"Maybe we can talk some evening." But Kelley was never free in the evening to visit. By the end of the winter he hated the evenings and the people who arrived by habit and sat in his living room until almost midnight.

After that winter Kelley moved with discretion into a new neighborhood. But even then, two winters ago he had left an old preacher in his cottage and had returned to find the man standing before an open shirt-drawer. The man had not seemed ashamed at being caught or even aware that he had been. He announced: "You have thirteen white shirts, six colored and twenty-three sports shirts." Kelley, therefore, respected and even envied the way in which Mr. Beattle, through training and temperament, managed to keep a proper distance.

Beattle, on his part, however, had learned slowly. He had had to break his lease in one house because an old couple there had tried to adopt him. They had insisted that he eat health foods with them, at least one meal a day. He could still taste with displeasure the dessert which was in-variably a protein marshmallow: dry cottage cheese rolled in wheat germ.

In turn, he had been too bold and enthusiastic in one of his own friendships. He had discovered in a bookstore a retired surgeon who had gone to school in Switzerland and spoke French with a beautiful accent. Later over a cup of mint tea they had continued the animated appraisals of Victor Hugo and Balzac, exchanged names and addresses, and after that he had gone often to the surgeon's to speak French. It was thoroughly delightful to Mr. Beattle and he did not realize that his companion was not as delighted as he until he was stopped one day on the stairway by the gentleman's landlady and told that the old surgeon was asleep and was not to be disturbed in the afternoons.

After that when they met, less often and by accident, they still had lively discussions, but Mr. Beattle could not enter into them with the same eagerness as before and was always somewhat apologetic toward the surgeon. The doctor was also apologetic: "I must rest a great deal because of this condition. But there's nothing to prevent us from having dinner together, is there?" The invitation and acceptances remained tenuous; and even when he read in the paper a notice of the surgeon's death, he could not believe wholeheartedly in the "condition" and still felt rebuffed.

Somewhat inadvertently the same thing had happened between Beattle and Kelley. In their early days on the porch the year before, they had talked a great deal about general topics and enough about private ones to give each a feeling of security and to satisfy a natural curiosity before it could exceed itself.

Beattle, for instance, knew that Mr. Kelley had made a comfortable fortune manufacturing metal office furniture, that his oldest son and son-in-law were managing the firm, that Mr. Kelley had been warned by his doctors to retire, and to lose a considerable amount of weight which he had been unable to do. Until her death twelve years ago, his wife had watched his diet and weight for him. He had always traveled a great deal, in North America, and always stayed at the best hotels and eaten the best that was offered. His cottage and patio in the back cost four times as much as Mr. Beattle's upstairs efficiency apartment and yet he felt that he was doing himself an injustice by not buying a house on the Inland Waterway, on the other coast, somewhere above Fort Lauderdale.

Kelley knew less about Mr. Beattle. He knew the man had never married, had previously lived with a sister and her family in a small university town where the brother-in-law was connected with the business part of the school, and that Mr. Beattle had never been head of the department and was, he could not hide the fact from Mr. Kelley who understood the necessity of promotions, in retrospect a little bitter. Kelley did not know and could not determine, but would not approach the subject even obliquely, what exactly Mr. Beattle used for money. He had written to his daughter and asked at the reference room of the library and had gathered that the retirement pay for an associate professor would be very small, less for instance than he himself paid in rent for the little cottage.

The incident which determined the limit of their relationship had not occurred on the porch; and neither of the men could have, at the moment, recalled or recognized it. It was almost nothing at all. One day last fall, Mr. Kelley had told Mr. Beattle that later in the afternoon his car, a two-year-old Cadillac, which had been in storage, would be checked thoroughly and brought to him. He had been rather pleased and said, "We won't have to depend on taxis now."

Mr. Beattle said that would be nice indeed, not realizing that he was included in the "we" since he never called cabs.

That evening he had been pressing a pair of trousers when there was a series of knocks on the door. He had only time to hide the iron in the oven and push the ironing board behind the bookcase so that it could not be seen from the entrance way, when the knocks sounded again and Mr. Kelley's deep voice calling: "Mr. Beattle!"

When he opened the door, Mr. Kelley was breathing heavily but managed to say that the car was out on the street, to come, they would go to an uptown bar together. Mr. Beattle was intent on sniffing the air for the smell of scorched wool and stared at Mr. Kelley blankly. Mr. Kelley had repeated the invitation. Mr. Beattle had thought to himself: "Two dollars for a round and then I'll have to buy him a drink and that'll be my groceries for almost two days." He had declined.

Kelley had gone down the steps, holding to the banisters with both hands, thinking of people he could and should have asked. After all, he and Mr. Beattle were merely porch-acquaintances through necessity. "Still, he could have asked me in." He held to the newel post. "At least till I could get my breath." By the time he reached his car he had thought of a couple he knew who would appreciate a ride along the bay shore and had forgotten Mr. Beattle. But it never occurred to him to ask him anywhere again.

Beattle, on his side, did not feel that he could afford any sort of entertainment. Once every three weeks he bought a fifth of bourbon and had one drink a day, not before dinner, but in the middle of the evening when he knew that if he did not talk to someone he might go insane. Usually he would talk, then, to himself, sometimes in French, sometimes in English, rarely in both. About twice a year he would go on to a second and third drink and finish an entire pint or more. On such occasions he would sing French student songs and dance with a chair and finally fall across the bed giggling and sleep with his clothes on. The next day he would smile fondly at the image of himself dancing and sleeping with his clothes on.

"There he is!" Kelley sat upright in the chaise longue. The postman's shrill whistle could be heard intermittently far up the boulevard. He had still to come to the corner, go up and down the one-way side street, before arriving; but the first sound of his whistle was always the cue for the two men on the porch to begin talking again.

On the other porches other people were gathering. An old man in the park stopped, still bent, lifted his head, and listened. When the whistle blew again, he turned about on his cane in a small half-circle and in tiny scraping steps headed back toward the houses, stopping to listen and to rest and to wipe his forehead with a folded handkerchief from his breast pocket. Soon the park was empty. Only one woman in a crocheted hat dozed on a bench in the sun, her dark glasses slipping down on her sharp nose, her cat on a chain, crouching watching a bird.

"I won't get anything today," Mr. Beattle said. One of them and sometimes both of them felt compelled to make the statement every day. It was a charm that brought them luck. Then they could be surprised or feign an indifference to hide their disappointment.

"I should," Mr. Kelley said. "I haven't had any in four days. Not even a post card."

The whistle was sharper now and more frequent. They tried not to pause when it blew, but in spite of their efforts it punctuated their conversation which became more and more animated.

"Still I have to wait," Mr. Beattle said. "Even when I know there's nothing."

Neither of them would use the expression which was heard everywhere that old people gathered: on the benches, in the grocery, at the laundry-store, in the post office, the park and at the barbershop: "It gives me something to do."

"I wish he would come early and get it over with," Mr. Kelley said. "I sleep as late as possible." He had never admitted this before; he listened to the whistle near the corner and went on: "If I wake before six, I take another sleeping pill. Generally I can sleep till after ten."

"I wake at seven every morning," Mr. Beattle said. He'd always had nine o'clock classes.

"Seven!" Mr. Kelley said in admiration and pity. "What do you find to do all morning?" He had not meant to ask and his voice dropped on the word "morning" as though he were trying to negate the question.

Mr. Beattle seemed glad to answer. At least he spoke quickly: "Read. I read." He did not want to say that he swept, and dusted, and dusted his books, and once a week cleaned his typewriter, and cooked lunch and brushed his clothes and spot-cleaned them with damp cloths and naph-thas and pressed his drip-dry shirts. All these things he felt would be admitting poverty and Mr. Kelley, with his maid who came twice a week, would think them beneath a man's dignity. "And do research," he said, a little pompously.

The word "research" and the tone annoyed Mr. Kelley and again he felt the need to offend Mr. Beattle. "I stay in bed as long as possible. Then I get up." Kelley waited for the postman's whistle which was on the side street now. "And stand naked in front of the mirror. Sometimes I even pull up a chair and sit naked in front of it for fifteen or twenty minutes."

Mr. Beattle rolled his cane along the arms of the chair and glanced uncomfortably at Mr. Kelley.

"It keeps me from getting off my diet," Mr. Kelley said, gratified at having roused Mr. Beattle. "Then I make my shower last as long as I can." The postman blew again, only three houses away. "Breakfast takes me over an hour with the paper and my coffee."

The postman was too near for conversation. Again, by agreement, they sank back into a silence. Mr. Beattle continued to roll his cane up and down the chair arms. Mr. Kelley rebuttoned two buttons on his shirt. The postman blew again and came up their walk and was now on their steps. He called out the mail as he sorted it between his fingers and dropped it into the five boxes under the awning. "Mr. Beattle, Dr. Beattle, Mr. Kelley, Mrs. McGuire, Mr. Johnston, Dr. Beattle, Mr. Thackston . . ."

"Thackston's moved!" Kelley said.

"Right." The postman picked the letter out of the box. "McGuire and Johnston and that's all." He swung his leather bag back over his hip and started down the steps.

"That's all?" Mr. Kelley asked.

"What're you complaining about?" the postman called from the walk. "You got one."

Mr. Beattle already standing was trying not to seem hasty.

"Did I get something?" Mr. Kelley asked.

"He called your name," Mr. Beattle said. He opened the door and stood on the top step picking his letters out.

"Would you hand me mine?" Mr. Kelley asked in a voice that still showed doubt.

Beattle handed him an envelope without glancing at it. Beattle sat down before he began studying his own three pieces. One was from a modern language group and he knew it would be asking for money. One was from a former student who was now teaching and with whom he carried on a regular correspondence even though he could not exactly recall the man's face or appearance or work. The third was a post card from his sister. He would take them all upstairs and read them over a cup of tea.

Mr. Kelley was plundering his envelope, Beattle noticed, in the way a small boy would open a box of chocolate crackers. Kelley read without glasses, holding the letter some distance away and to one side. He was grinning and once he laughed. "Well, well," he looked up at Beattle as though he were a stranger, "my baby grandson's walking now!"

"That's what babies eventually do, isn't it?" Beattle thought, but immediately censored himself for the envy he was feeling. He said nothing and waited for Mr. Kelley to finish his letter.

"Walking!" Mr. Kelley said again. He saw the look with which Mr. Beattle had repressed his feelings. "It's from my daughter-in-law," Mr. Kelley said. He was amused. "She begins: 'There's no news.' " He crammed the letter into his pocket with the wadded handkerchief.

"How old is he?" Mr. Beattle asked.

"Ten months. Walking. She says he's been walking for two weeks," Mr. Kelley said. "He was just learning to pull up the last time I saw him. Well . . ." he said. He looked across the park at the boats in the sun. "I'll have to send him something."

"Shoes perhaps," Mr. Beattle said.

Mr. Kelley laughed but at the same time he thought: "I shouldn't have told him."

"Maybe a little boat," Mr. Kelley said. He thought about it and tried to remember where he had seen a splendid toy boat. He would ask one of the youngsters on the dock. When he thought of the youngsters he remembered their sneakers and that he had seen in the dime store red sneakers for babies, not as long as the width of his hand. "Shoes, that's not a bad idea," he said.

Mr. Beattle felt pleased with himself and no longer envious in the least. He pulled himself up and stood with his cane poised and watched Mr. Kelley seem to spread out in the sun which slanted across the chaise longue.

"Are you going to the grocery?" Mr. Beattle asked. It was, in essence, an invitation since he was standing nearer to the glass door than to the hallway.

"Not today," Mr. Kelley said, folding his hands across his ponderous stomach. "I think I might doze awhile." He watched Mr. Beattle going down the boulevard, swinging his cane in perfect unison with his left leg, and watched the palms swaying in the park, and beyond the park, the masts swaying and the youngsters still jumping from the boats to the docks and back again. He let his eyes close for a moment and could still see the white sails and the seagulls wheeling in the bright sun.

WHERE SHE
BRUSHED HER HAIR

Here in San Francisco the other night we had a party for a friend of ours, a psychiatrist from New York. It was a very bad party: we had invited some psychiatrists and analysts whom we did not know really well, and too many European-born doctors who made the party formal instead of relaxed. They did not drink enough and instead of crowding together in one room, as people do at good parties, they arranged themselves in isolated groups throughout the large rooms which could have held, Kathy whispered to me in passing, three times as many people.

The party was from six to eight and we had expected many of the fifty people to be here until ten or even until midnight. But it wasn't that kind of party. By eight-thirty everyone was gone and Kathy and I were exhausted; a sure sign it was an unsuccessful party.

Suddenly the doorbell rang and Howard and Eve Bryant

came back in. They had been the first to leave but they had decided, after looking for a restaurant, that our ham was exactly what they wanted: a ham sandwich each and cold shrimp.

We were pleased for they were the best people to talk over a party with. Eve and Kathy had been in school together and Howard was easy to talk to and made jokes, the sort of analyst everyone said about: "He doesn't seem like a psychiatrist at all."

The party had troubled him. He'd felt attacked by our New York psychiatrist on several grounds and levels and he wanted to talk. There is nothing that can make a person feel so sane as to comfort a socially wounded psychiatrist; and so after we had eaten ham sandwiches and made fresh coffee, Kathy and Eve went into the living room to gossip and giggle in a schoolgirlish way which they never either do with anyone else.

Howie and I moved through the double doorway to my office which tonight had been the bar and there with Irish coffee Howie talked until he'd got all his grievances out and had begun to make jokes about them. It had been an unfortunate gathering of people.

Then, as usual, we began to talk about fiction and fiction-writing which seemed to fascinate him more than talk about therapy.

I said: "But why is it that stories have value and people will pay for them and yet everyone is bored by dreams?"

"Bored by dreams!" He could not believe me.

"Maybe not if it's your business," I said, "but I am. I hate to hear dreams. I hate the singsong voice people use to tell them. The monotone. The trancelike stupid look that blanks out all expression in their eyes."

He could not believe I was being serious.

"You can't be serious," he kept saying, which of course was enough to make me exaggerate my boredom. "But you might try, Claude," he said patiently, "just once: writing down your dream and thinking about it and seeing what a story it really is."

We talked on for a long while about authors who had killed themselves and how it could have been predicted, or in some cases could not, from their work, and about Marilyn Monroe and the effect of her death on patients; and then he would come back to dreams and say: "I would suggest you try it. You would, I believe, find it interesting."

I promised him several times I would; and at the gate shook hands with him in promise.

That night I made a special effort to remember my dream when I waked before dawn; and as a result, the next morning was able to record the following:

Dream

The mother is kneeling before her dresser brushing her long black hair steadily, with even strong strokes; caught up in the rhythm of her movements, her thoughts turned inward, her face toward the black silk cloth she has thrown over the rug. She is unaware that anyone is in the room, for indeed, since I am invisible and omniscient, there is not. The door from the dressing room to the bedroom begins to open, and I the dreamer think, no, that is too soon for the door to open; that is only the first two pages of the story; as always you're taking the pace too fast; four more pages should pass before anyone enters, then keep that pace throughout the rest of the story. The door closes and the mother continues, alone, brushing her hair, while I, invisible, watch.

First Thoughts

When I first wake I know that I have stated clearly my most serious problem as a short story writer. Having come at story telling through writing ten-line feature stories for newspapers, I tend to rush through scenes without draining them, without exploring and exploiting the emotions. In addition, and perhaps more important than training is a quirk of temperament; I am afraid of boring readers, losing them by not being instantly likeable, and showing them immediately that there will be action. Only recently have I realized that in my own reading it is not action I like but the musing about the action. The dream, I believe, is trying to teach me something about the pace of a short story, the sexual tension and building and resolution, if you like. But my mind is open—for, perhaps, and most likely, the dream is about something altogether different and has nothing to do with fiction. At any rate, but preferably the slow rate suggested in the dream, to find the true meaning of the dream, let us begin:

The Story

All day she has been anticipating a visitor this evening and the house is ready for the unannounced guest, the food cooked, the table set.

At last it is five o'clock and the mother is alone. She is kneeling on a square of black taffeta which she has used for this purpose all her married life. She was married in 1910 when she was twenty, now it is 1930 and she is forty. Anyone watching her in the dressing room, with the late afternoon sun fractured into rainbows by the stained-glass window of the Victorian house, would think she was trying to gather up the rainbow pieces, or was about to pray, or that a religious rite is about to begin. And in a sense it is, for the things which Ardella Perry learned when she was a little girl—Ardella Phillips then ("Change the name but not the letter/Change for worse and not for better")—she is faithful to as to a catechism.

Two of these precepts she is keeping faith with now even though each day the faith grows harder to keep. The first and most important is that a lady or gentleman must have at least one hour to himself each day. Her own mother, born in 1845 and married at twenty, the last year of the Confederacy, had always insisted on this hour from five to six each day for herself and for her four daughters. It made no difference what each chose to do during that hour in so far as they were not within sight of each other, not making noise or calling out, and not engaged in activity which was like the endless work they pursued during the rest of the day.

"Leisure time" Mamma had said and "Mamma" was pronounced not at all Southern and slow, but quickly and with a rising lilt the way Ardella's grandmother had admired children saying to their mothers, before the War, in Paris. "Leisure time, you must learn to use it as ladies do: needlework, not darning and mending, mind you, but pretty work—crocheting, tatting, embroidery." There was something Mamma felt was common about knitting, and even though they were as poor as all their upcountry Carolina neighbors, and needed knitted stockings just as badly, during that hour of privacy they never knitted. "Read: the Bible, Shakespeare, *The Almanac,* Scott . . . or better still, think. Reflect. A lady needs to reflect. Look back over the day to see if she has in haste offended anyone, has failed to be kind where kindness was needed. And when isn't it needed? Well, there are people who will abuse kindness and take it for weakness, and it is your duty to teach these people, who lack training, to distinguish." Mamma had now been dead since 1904, and yet Ardella, picking up the bone-handled comb from the towel, can hear every soft word as clearly as if they were still living in the overseer's house on the edge of what had once been Grandpapa Moore's plantation.

Ardella throws her long black hair over her head. It is damp from being wrapped in a towel during her bath, and the breeze from the sleeping-porch window feels cool from her neck all the way to her waist where even the ends have felt heavy in the heat.

The house is quiet for a moment, as if a baby were asleep. The twins are still at the library and music. The two small girls are at peace with their game of Pollyanna on the side porch beneath the sleeping porch. Such moments are rare and in such moments she realizes how fast time and her life are going by. And she, she has so little time to herself she hardly knows any longer who she is. She is the house, the children, her husband, the trucks, the vegetable garden; she is all these things that occupy her waking hours, so that like a dreamer she is all things and nowhere, every person and yet alone. It is only when she comes here to comb and brush her hair, not a hundred strokes, but a thousand, that she persuades her soul back into her body, recoups her strength, apportions her energy to the one most in need of it at the moment, thanks her God for her magnificent body and vitality, her appetite, digestion, and health. This is the gift for which she is most thankful and where does health show to better advantage than in a beautiful head of hair? Where, even the Bible asks, is a woman's glory?

How does Nola, she wonders, stand her head bound up even on the hottest days. She likes much that is old-fashioned about Nola, her beautiful manners, but on these days she should be bareheaded. Her temper would improve, Mrs. Perry feels sure.

This morning she had started to mention it again but had not gotten very far. Sometimes Nola knew what she was going to say and stopped her with a glance. She had begun and got no further than "Nola, it's going to be another hot day."

Nola nodded, unsmiling.

Mrs. Perry had not slept well at all and already she had made coffee and cut the biscuits, still on the dough board, before the cook, still in her hat, let herself in, humming a comforting song, neither jazz nor church, to herself. Nola said simply good morning and nothing more while taking off her hat and pinning on her head cloth. Mrs. Perry was standing, coffee cup in hand, trying to recapture the dream which troubled her sleep and finally waked her. Whatever the dream—it eluded her completely now—she had waked with the sense that someone was coming today.

"Somebody," she says, trying to be cheerful in the face of Nola's sullenness, "is coming . . ."

"For dinner?" Nola asks, ready to be all day cantankerous if more work is added.

"I don't know. I feel like we should be ready."

Nola says nothing but turns her back as she pours her tin cup of coffee.

Mrs. Perry is quick to avoid trouble: "We'll just have Sunday's dinner tonight. Sunday you can take off."

Nola is partially mollified but considers first the idea, then the taste of the coffee. She approves of neither: "You sure don't know anything about making coffee. You got to use a lot of grounds to make good coffee. That's one thing you can't skimp on." She implies a criticism of the way the house is lately being run. "Depression or no Depression."

Mrs. Perry has suspected the coffee did not taste right. "Make another pot and I'll drink this."

The two women know just how far to push, how far to pamper each other, and establish their working relationship for the day before the husband and children come down to breakfast.

"Company," Nola says, pouring the weak coffee into a saucepan. "But you don't know who."

"I'll invite Deliah and we'll kill a chicken and if no one shows up we'll simply call it Sunday dinner."

"On Friday night?" Nola says. She allows a musical tone of amusement to well up in her throat.

Mrs. Perry considers herself, as everyone else considers her, a sensible woman. Yet she does listen to her feelings, and more often than not to her presentiments because they (as they are apt to with strong-willed women) do come true.

With thick coffee brewing, the biscuits in the gas oven, Nola feels better. They talk about Deliah, Mr. Perry's sister whom they both adore, and then again Nola feels annoyed. "I suppose you're going to want me to stick around here until after dinner."

"Not if it's only Deliah."

Nola sighs. She feels the need to re-establish the fact that this is not her day for work, much less for company-work. Mention of Deliah takes her out of herself for a while, but now she descends again to her depths. She comes to the surface for a moment when the fresh coffee begins to percolate. "I'd leave have one day off next week, 'stead of Sunday," she says.

To Mrs. Perry it is all the same.

In the face of such easy victory Nola feels the need to explain her mood and request. "I think I'll be wanting me a day of rest come Tuesday or Wednesday."

Now it is clear, Nola's impatience and irritability of the past few days. Mrs. Perry wishes the younger woman would take aspirin or something at such times instead of upsetting the entire household, bossing the children around, burning everything in the oven.

A glimpse of the dream comes to Mrs. Perry: she herself was standing at the sink letting water run out the drain. In the sink, somewhere in the rushing water, was a translucent grape and she was trying to capture it before it went down the drain. In the peculiar values of dreams the grape was more valuable than a pearl. Almost than life itself; and frantically, though no one else in the kitchen had guessed her panic, she tried to cup the elusive grape in her calm hands. . . .

"I dreamed last night . . ." she begins and Nola who is fascinated by dreams holds still, the coffeepot in one hand, and listens to the dream with a face as blank and flittingly troubled as the face of a dreamer. Nola's free hand cups the grape in sympathy with the dream woman.

"I wouldn't want me a dream like that," she says after considerable reflection. She shakes the dream from her head and ears. "No sir-ree . . ."

"Why?" Mrs. Perry asks.

"I just wouldn't," Nola says. "That's all."

Mrs. Perry knows she must allow Nola her time of mystery which may be five minutes or half the day before pressing for an answer.

"I don't think it means anything," Mrs. Perry says. She is looking out the window: "I thought I staked those pea-vines."

"They grow fast," Nola says as Mrs. Perry walks onto the side porch. The peas are a concession to the Depression. Vegetables are appearing now among the flowers: radishes in the petunias, carrots and parsley with the summer-snow, turnip greens beyond the alyssum.

Mrs. Perry walks down the gravel drive, through the iron gateway to the front yard. Here under the water oaks there is not yet a breeze and the fragrance of wistaria binding the porch is too heady, almost nauseating. She retreats to the gravel drive and back yard again. The coffee is undrinkable. She sets the cup on the porch and wonders why she feels so strongly the approach of a visitor.

She makes out a list in her head for the day: the twins,

Moore to his music lesson, Marcia to tennis and the library. That gets the twins out of the way for the afternoon. She'll keep the little ones with her, sweeping the front walk and porch, running the wax mop over the dark, stained floors. She glances up at the peeling paint on the house. She has saved $83 to have it painted, and Mr. John Brown will scrape and paint it and repair the sagging steps, side and back, and repair all broken gutters and window cords for $125. He has come back last week and agreed since money is now so hard to come by, to do it for one hundred even, same paint, two coats like he said. But she feels $125 was the set price and intends to pay him that. The poor man has begged and she has finally agreed to pay in installments. When she has saved $100 he can commence; and she will pay him the $25 later. He wants to start immediately but they both know the $17 is not going to be easy to save. And in case of sickness which costs money, she will not be obliged to him.

Douglas Perry and Deliah were born in the house, in the very bed where her four children were born and Mrs. Perry loves the place. She makes no changes in it. All she does in the way of spending is for replacing (velvet draperies in the parlor, wooden blinds across the front); or for refinishing (floors scraped, brass chandeliers and brass doorknobs and name plate and numerals polished and reshellacked); or restoring (ivy pulled off the brick retaining walls and walks, trees pruned back, daisies planted to hide the legginess of the old shrubbery, rehanging the iron gates). Douglas and Deliah are amused by her respect for the place. But even they are becoming proud of it again. Now Marcia is taking an interest and before fall the tennis court may again have lines on it and a net of sorts. The Depression may last a lifetime but there is no excuse, she feels lately, in letting it depress children. Lately she has felt strong and her voice, she hopes, has that calm, confidential tone of Roosevelt's. If she can make Douglas have faith in himself and his own strength! He and Deliah used to be the ones with a real joy about them. Well, Deliah, in spite of Claude's death, still has. And Douglas has when Deliah is there and the children; but at night she sometimes has to hold him very tight and even then in his silences he seems to tremble. She has been poor almost all her life, but Douglas is not used to it. "What about the children?" he asks.

"I'd rather bring them up poor and with manners than running wild, rich." She is not criticizing his upbringing, because no family in town was ever more conservative and deliberately inconspicuous than his. She herself was taught by her mother to be proud poor, and with good manners and morals, the two were inseparable and rightly so.

"You can make up for having no garnets and sapphires by the way you hold your head and speak and move your hands," Mamma said when they complained. People who didn't know them thought from the balance of their heads, the steadiness of their eyes (not staring, simply not seeing) that they were haughty and were always delighted to hear the rich, but well modulated laughter which could come from the long throats of the Phillips girls. "You can judge a person by the way he laughs and by the way he accepts gifts." Mrs. Perry could hear her mother's voice. "And women, you can judge how they respect themselves by the way they respect their hair. Let a man not shave and let a woman not tend to her hair and you may know they are headed for trouble." Trouble, why was hers breaking now and coming out in such drifts?

Mrs. Perry begins the rhythmic strokes. She seizes the great cataract of hair at the scalp and draws her left hand, which barely reaches around the coil, slowly down it. The right hand with the British brush follows close behind and as the right hand reaches the tip, the left has already gathered the hair springing from the scalp and is drawing it again into an abundant rope. Again the brush starts at the nape of her neck, comes over the crown, and down the long, constrained rope of hair. Over and over until the rhythm is hypnotic. Occasionally she loses balance and tips forward toward the black taffeta square, but her body has the strength and skill of a dancer's and without a change in rhythm she straightens herself, and continues in the rhythm that soothes her mind and body.

She claims an hour to herself and is lucky to be granted thirty minutes. But some days for an hour she is allowed to return to the center of her being, to refind herself, to gather herself and her strength together, to be for one continuous time not . . .

"Mama." The door is pushed open. Hannah, her baby girl, is standing there, at three already apologetic in a nice way, not cowering, simply aware she is intruding but feeling too strongly the need to. Hannah smiles winningly and when the smile is not returned she knows this is her mother's time to herself, thinks hard for something to say.

The mother holds back the weight of the hair with her entire forearm and looks under the arc at the child. "Yes, Hannah." Later she will be warm with the girl, make up for her coolness now.

Hannah has found something to say: "I think Baby Brother's awake."

She must be firm with Hannah even though Hannah has thought of such a charming story to gain admission. "No, Hannah, I don't think the baby is awake." Baby Brother is the new name for Hannah's soldier-doll.

"I think he needs you." Hannah continues as if her story has not been refuted.

"Maybe the baby girl does," the mother smiles at her, "not the baby boy."

Hannah is ready, almost on tiptoes, to run to her and squeeze the life out of her with love. Of all the children

Hannah is the one who can wreck herself each day with some emotion too strong for her young soul to bear.

"Mother will be out soon. You and Cindy keep clean."

Cindy, six, is standing now behind Hannah. Cindy is the little mother. If they are not shooed from the room, Cindy will find excuses to be in, straightening the bureau, making a great fuss over the tangle-balls of hair on the bureau, finding some excuse to be maid to her mother, to get her hands on the comb and brush. Today she is too tired to let Cindy even try to brush her hair, no, that would make her too nervous, today. Cindy refuses to have her own hair trimmed and already has demanded a comb and brush for Christmas. But Cindy's hairbrushing is at night and she still needs her mother's help with it. She considers it only fair play to help her mother in return.

"If you want to help me," the mother says, "see that you and Hannah stay clean till they get here."

"Can we help Nola?" Cindy is at the stage where it is hard to keep her out from under foot in the kitchen. Later when she is as old as Marcia and can be of help, she, like Marcia, will find excuses to go to the library, knowing that an education will take precedence over any domestic emergency.

"Nola is in the yard," the mother says. "In the yard" means resting, for it is under the fig tree that Nola has her own outdoor sitting room: two rush-bottomed chairs and a wicker bench. Here near the back gate she can receive visits from other cooks and nursemaids, and occasionally delivery boys. Their voices are part of the summer music and soothe the household. Baby-sitting is not part of Nola's rest period, for if the mother recognizes the need for an hour to herself, she demands it for Nola too. How long they can continue to pay Nola she does not know and Nola will not listen to any talk that she should accept other offers.

"Can we go visit Nola?" the children want to know.

"Did she invite you?"

"Yes!" Hannah lies immediately, joyfully, now that the idea has been invented.

Cindy, though older, is confused by Hannah's outright lie: "Not exactly. She doesn't know we want to see her."

The mother punishes them both with a short glance. "If she didn't invite you, you can't go."

The children seem smaller after her admonishment and she will later make lemonade for them if there is time but there probably will not be. She bends to her brushing again and is dizzy. She shuts her eyes to still the carpet.

"You go only where you are invited and you stay for meals if you are invited the day before." They are her words, her mother's words, her grandmother's words and are worn smooth by three generations of use. Even Hannah sometimes mocks her with them, behind her back to be sure, and she is pleased not annoyed when Hannah does. What you teach a child before it is five . . .

"The guineas, the guineas are laying somewhere," Ardella's mother says. They have eaten lunch at the iron table built around the trunk of the cherry tree; for now while the tree is in bloom, and later in leaf shade through the heat of summer, they will picnic here at noon.

Her mother's words mean no more to Ardella than the clucking of the brood hen, the laughter of the ducks, the song of the morning-glory. Mockingbird, if she stops she knows morning-glory from mockingbird but the song is both. Her mother's words are repeated by her mother again; and again by Ardella's own silent lips but she is no longer eating buttered corn bread, she is standing in front of the furniture store in town five miles away and staring at the doll, a Confederate soldier. Ardella owns no real doll. Cindy is a sock-doll stuffed with cotton from the old Phillips plantation . . .

"Mother, can we have . . ." the real Cindy speaks still,

thirty years later, at the door. Listen to the needs of children, not to the words but what is actually being asked for ". . . one piece of gingerbread each."

"One piece each and that's all." They must learn the meaning of privacy; and for themselves, later, the need for it. "And shut the door now, Cindy, Hannah."

"Who is coming?" Cindy asks for the tenth time that day.

"I really don't know," the mother says. "If no one else, your Aunt Deliah."

"And Uncle Claude!" Hannah cries.

"Uncle Claude is dead!" Cindy says in horror. At six she does not understand death any better than does Hannah but she has learned in three months not to mention him, especially in front of Aunt Deliah.

"Uncle Claude will be here!" Hannah announces emphatically.

"Mother!" Cindy needs help or she may be convinced by Hannah.

"Children," the mother says, "shut the door."

She can hear the children explaining to each other the realities of their beliefs as they go down the long back stairs to the butler's pantry.

Hannah! One might as well argue with a gatepost, persuade a turnip. The poor man was not two days in his grave before she'd named her boy doll "Uncle Claude." Quite by chance she discovered she can say "Uncle Claude" if she claims it is her khaki doll she's talking about. But recently the doll has become "Brother Doll" and the mother hopes the name will last for the duration of Deliah's visit this evening.

The small dressing room, with the door to the bedroom shut, seems unduly hot and to open the outside door to the sleeping porch is to invite not only heat from the late afternoon sun but also more demands, from Nola, the twins, even from her husband should he have received her message at his office and arrived home early in anticipation of a guest who might turn out to be nothing more than—her own desire for company, her instinct telling her everyone needs a small party at the end of this particularly humid and tiring week tinged with growing poverty? She says to herself:

"Poor . . ." but before she knows what she intends to think, the heat, the closeness of the room has felled her and she is on all fours, crouched over the black taffeta, now a prayer-rug. For a moment she must lie down.

She shuts her eyes and the street traffic is as distant and soft as wind in a forest and the back gate swinging idly on its hinges sings like, she knows but does not want to know . . . why can't Nola be persuaded to latch it after herself . . . sings like . . . a nausea threatens her throat and she shuts her eyes . . . Nola, latch the gate, the gate, latch it for God's sake . . . sings like . . . it's too late, let it swing, let it sing . . . like the rattlesnake. . . .

She is lying under the brush pile now and before her are the guinea eggs, a hundred of them, a thousand. Already she has filled her apron with the ones from the near edge but as far as she can see under the brush pile are eggs, eggs, and more eggs. Small brown guinea eggs. For each dozen her mother will give her a nickel and for twenty dozen a dollar. And for a dollar the Confederate doll will be hers to take out of the store window, to hold on the way home, sitting on her pillow on the back of the wagon.

"Mamma," she wants to scream, "Mamma, I've found where the guinea hens are laying." But her mother with her two baskets, one for wild strawberries, one for mushrooms, has long ago disappeared into the forest and young ladies do not scream. She tries to count the eggs but they come together, double, treble, she counts the same egg twice and pretends not to notice the hissing is growing stronger and stronger. First it is far away, then it is near. Now it is everywhere. As if each egg is singing a dry rattling song.

She knows the noise; she knows what it means. Yet by
an order to herself, she does not look away from the eggs
which she is reaching for as far as her ten-year-old sum-
mer-brown arms will reach. She crawls deeper under the
brush. She follows her hands gathering the eggs as if her
hands were kittens to be sneaked up on, caught, dragged
back to her bosom. And all the time the silky sliding rattle
which she orders herself not to hear.

She sees the doll in the store window; she sees herself
holding it on the wagon; she cannot quite see herself with
the doll at home, in the house. On the porch she sees herself hiding there with the doll, waiting behind the boxwoods
for the Yankees, the Cherokees, for all mortal enemies, she
and the soldier protecting them all from all evil.

Again she slides forward, dragging carefully the apron-
bag by its neck. Now she is under the center of the brush
pile and one way out is as short as another. Above the
eggs, above the place where she sees the doll in the window, and on the porch a branch creaks heavily, something
heavy drops to a lower branch, the pile shifts and seems all
to move. The silky droning stops then starts again, moving
slowly as the brush pile seems to slide. She is looking into
the eyes of the snake itself, nearer, ever nearer, till death
do us part. Her hands move out again, toward the eggs,
obeying again the unvoiced command from that unknown
part of her which will have the doll at any price. Two more
eggs, two more. The head of the snake weaves from side to
side. The thick body coils through the brush toward the
nest. Now it is a moral battle: the eggs must be rescued,
saved from the snake. Now the eggs have the love with-
drawn from the soldier doll. Now she is a mother rescuing
her young from all terror. Two more eggs and two more
and the snake has reached the far edge of the nest and
dangles its head above the eggs. Cautiously, two more and

she will crawl backward, and drag the apron-bundle of eggs after her, and place them safely near the spring and run to her mother, slowing to a ladylike walk, where the mother is kneeling ladylike, bending at the knees, not from the waist, turning the perfect leaves, picking the little berries which will be served with sugar tonight. Approaching softly saying softly, "Mamma, I have found the guinea nest where the guinea hens are laying. Saturday when we go to town, I will have money . . ." No snake. No. No snake. No.

The darting tongue flickers, fast as a bee wing, the head holds still, the thick body begins its coil for strength and spring. Two more eggs. That is enough. That is enough. Twice more the hands go out and twice more back and are moving forward again when the snake strikes and misses, its thick body smashing the eggs, thrashing over the broken eggs, through the brush.

Back, back, she scrambles back screaming without a sound from her dry lips. No snake. No. She is out from under the brush. No snake. No. She is running. No snake. She has the apron with her and the eggs are dropping out one by one. No. She holds them to her bosom and saves them. No snake. Blind with panic she has entered the woods, and blind and deaf she is when she walks into her strolling mother. No. No. No. Now, for the first time she breathes.

The picture is gone and under her on the floor is the black taffeta. The ivory handle of the brush is wet in her hand. She cannot push herself back to her kneeling position. For a moment, only for a moment longer she will lie here on the floor. The children cannot see her and will not be tempted to copy her. She is thankful for the thick carpet under her and feels better. The dizziness passes and with it all further knowledge of that day some thirty years before. Did she get the doll? She cannot remember it if she did.

She seems to remember looking at it again in the store window and thinking: "It is not the same doll." They cannot persuade her to buy it. It is not at any rate the doll her heart was set on.

Or is she confusing herself with Hannah and the khaki soldier doll? Hannah drags it around and has no maternal feeling for it at all. No, if she had got a doll she would have loved it and remembered it. Maybe there had not been money enough for them to buy the eggs. Or to please them she had said she no longer wanted the doll she, before, had wanted more than anything in the world.

Now the twins are back from music and the library. Moore is at the piano, the music bench slams shut; half-heartedly he runs a scale and midway breaks into a hymn and from there a waltz. Marcia is hitting a tennis ball against the side of the carriage house, mainly to annoy Nola on the other side, who is hollering at her to desist. Those two and their arguing, she is not sure she can take much of it this summer.

The horn of the A-model sounds in the shady back street and the gravel sprays as he turns, as usual, too fast into the driveway. "Douglas, one of these days a child is going to be playing there and you . . ."

But now she must get up. It is as if she had been asleep in the hammock and is stiff from cold. She rolls over on the floor and rises unsteadily to her feet. Already so late. Douglas home. Maybe the visitor is with him.

"Aunt Deliah! Deliah!" First Hannah begins and then the others, even the twins. Already before Deliah is out of the car it is a party. There'll be something, if no more than a balloon for every one of them, including Nola and Douglas and herself. Deliah never forgets anyone. A constrictor of jealousy tightens for only a second around her heart as she glances from the sleeping porch and sees Deliah being pulled by not one but all the children. It is a game and even Douglas laughs as he tries to rescue his sister. Ardella has forgotten Douglas's laugh, she hears it so seldom lately. Tonight though will be a party!

With the children diverted and Douglas and Deliah together, she takes her time dressing. Dressed, and with a linen towel about her shoulders, she coils the hair about her wrist and lets it slip over her head to be pinned with large celluloid pins to the crown of her head. She studies her face, glowing from heat and the exertion of arranging her hair, and thinks how strange that only a few minutes before she was lying on the floor in her dressing shift. She gathers the cloud of hair and rolls it into a ball before letting it float into the wicker basket.

She stands too quickly and the blood leaves her head. She reaches for the door to the bedroom and unsteadily approaches the bed. "I'll lie down, just for a second," she thinks, and when she opens her eyes again the room is darker, the house quieter. She has dozed off and now is waking.

Moore and Deliah are playing a duet. She listens. No, how strange: it is not Moore; it is Douglas and Deliah. As she listens a peace, deeper than any she has known for a long time, fills her as she lies there. ". . . Gone are the cares from life's early toil . . ." now their voices rise to her. On the side porch the children are whispering, plotting some mischief for the table. The children move off to plot with Nola on the back porch; and downstairs the singing breaks off and only one person, Douglas, begins an etude, simply, lightly, as if his mind is on a hummingbird.

Ardella rises carefully and this time is not made dizzy by standing. She reaches the top step and, lest the vertigo return, descends carefully the wide, carpeted front stairs. Before she is all the way down, she hears, not meaning to, Deliah's voice, rich and musical: "She's so beautiful when she's pregnant. I knew by her face, the glow . . ."

Ardella pauses and automatically places a protective hand over her stomach. "Pregnant?" She feels herself flushing. The knowledge fills every cell of her body at once.

"Why hasn't she told me?" Douglas finds the right, light touch for each note. "It makes me . . ."

"Jealous!" Deliah cries. "Oh Douglas! I know, I know!"

"How long . . . when?" the music falters, stops.

"I don't know. But the morning we buried Claude I knew by a grim, angry look about her face before a year she would have another, that she would replace Claude. There's a certain wonderful type of woman who will always fight death with birth."

For an instant Ardella is tempted to flee back upstairs; but thinks incongruously, her hand still on her stomach: "There goes the house paint. Poor Mr. Brown. No. I promised him and I will." How? Why must they always guess before she allows herself to know? How long has she known without admitting it? She must stop them from saying more.

"Deliah!" she calls. "Douglas, didn't I promise you we'd have company today? Deliah . . . " With arms outstretched, her heart bursting with love for her widowed sister-in-law, her husband, the children, Nola, the entire vulnerable world, she enters the parlor.

And I, the dreamer, yet unborn, her last child, the unannounced guest, enter the room with her, having finally been allowed to share that hour of privacy which later was always denied to me when she brushed her hair.

Now, sitting here at my desk, I am confused. For the gate in the story is the iron gate my wife has just had repaired here in San Francisco; and the dressing room is not in the house where I grew up but here in this house where once in play I surprised my wife (my mother, my child); and the party—I begin to understand.

Again I return to the night of our party. Howie and I

stood up, still talking, and I opened the door to the living room. At the far end, between the candelabra on the low piano, Kathy and Eve, their fingers racing in a childish duet, were laughing when they glanced up at us.

At the moment I guessed from Kathy's radiance that she had told Eve her news; and I was merely feeling glad I had not mentioned to Howie anything about a baby. It seemed right it should be the news of women.

But now in memory, I stand there in awe; for I am the son who gained access to the dressing room; and I am the father who admitted jealousy of that son, who am I standing at the door, looking toward another unborn son (my father to be reborn?), who, too, am I; for I am the snake and the egg, the creator and the created; for I am the dreamer.